PRAISE FOR C

CH00921785

"*Chopping Spree* is a nost
and coming-of-age horror features. The blood-curdling
scares and betrayals will leave readers falling in line for
the funerary march to wealth, trapped in the killer scene
of capitalism. Fans of *Fear Street* and *You're Not Supposed
to Die Tonight* won't want to miss this."

—Haley Newlin, author of *Take Your Turn, Teddy*

"With its fast-paced story and twists, *Chopping Spree* is an
absolute masterclass in what a novella should be. I couldn't
put it down and devoured it in one sitting. If you ever
fantasized about a late-night party at an empty mall, Angela
Sylvaine's slasher will make you reconsider that dream."

—Jules V. Gachs, author of *Epiphany*

"*Chopping Spree* is equal parts a thrilling throwback
to pre-2000s teen slashers and a savage exploration of
modern socio-economic themes. Bursting off the page
with complex characters, shocking turns, and Angela
Sylvaine's swift cinematic writing, this is one nostalgic
trip to the mall you'll be glad you survived."

—Joey Powell, author of *Squirming All the Way Up* and
Editor-in-Chief at Mad Axe Media

"An explosive, fast-paced slasher that stabs the cult of
consumerism in the heart and twists the blade until
it bleeds."

—Yolanda Sfetsos, author of *Suffer the Darkness*

CHOPPING
SPREE

CONTENT WARNINGS

Violence, Murder, Kidnapping, Religious Extremism, Reference to the murder of a dog

Reader discretion is advised.

Edited by Rob Carroll
Book Design and Layout by Rob Carroll
Cover Art by Dan Fris
Cover Design by Rob Carroll

ISBN 978-1-958598-31-3 (paperback)
ISBN 978-1-958598-73-3 (eBook)

darkmatter-ink.com

CHOPPING
SPREE

ANGELA SYLVAINE

DARK
MATTER
INK

Thanks to all the final girls who inspire us to fight back against the monsters

ONE

PAUL GRIPPED THE window sash, hesitating. A pang of guilt cut through his gut at leaving his mom alone, at how much she'd worry if she got up and found his bed empty. But he needed a break, just for a few hours.

He slid open his window, inhaled the cleansing night air. Ellie was waiting for him.

A siren split the silence, and he froze. He waited for his mom to call out, but the house stayed quiet, and the siren tapered off, getting farther and farther away from their quiet, suburban neighborhood, where every house was a version of the next, and the lawns were kept perfectly mowed.

Paul pulled himself through the open window and hopped down, snagging his joggers on one of the rose bushes his mom once won awards for, but were now mostly dead. A thorn tore through his pants and bit into the front of his thigh, coming dangerously close to a very valuable piece of his anatomy.

"Shit." He watched as the dot of blood, appearing black under the light of the half moon, grew to the size of a quarter. Hissing at the sting, he pressed the heel of his hand to the wound, waited for the bleeding to subside. The pants would have to be trashed or his mom would think he was fighting again.

Paul closed the window with a silent prayer she wouldn't wake up. She'd stopped tiptoeing into his room at night to touch his shoulder, wake him up and make sure he was there, was real. Lately, she only peeked in, though he didn't hear the creak of the door, her muffled sobs. The line of pillows stuffed beneath his bedspread should do the trick if she paid him a visit.

Since his dick dad left, Paul was all she had. Just the two of them now, so they had to stick together, had to take care of each other, she said. But he was suffocating in that house, and the only person he could talk to waited for him at the park. Paul felt for the velvet pouch in his pocket, just one of those cheap little snap-in-half hearts that would probably tarnish within a month, but it was the best he could do on a five-finger discount. After track season was over, he'd get a job and buy Ellie something nice, something more like what she deserved.

He'd get something for his mom too.

Paul crossed the dewy grass, hiding behind the tree at the edge of the yard when a car passed, its headlights threatening to reveal him. He frowned. Hiding probably made him look much more suspicious, and he didn't need one of the neighbors calling the cops. Squaring his shoulders, he strode down the sidewalk, hands in his pockets, traveling from one pool of streetlight to the next. Just taking a walk, nothing shady here.

He crossed the street. Another block and he reached the edge of the park, which was across from another darkened neighborhood. He could just make out the playground in the distance, past the ball field. "Elliieee, bayyyybyyy," he sang under his breath, throat tightening in anticipation of her arms wrapped around him. He didn't care if they fooled around, just wanted to feel the warmth of her pressed to his chest, inhale the scent of her lavender shampoo.

Tires swished on pavement and headlights washed over him from behind. He kept walking, started to whistle, then stopped. *Calm down, you're trying too hard,* he thought.

The lights cut out, leaving him in darkness.

Paul looked behind him. A car—no—a van was parked at the curb. Motor still running. White with no markings on it that he could see.

He sped up, still walking, but fast, aimed for that next pool of streetlight. It's nothing, he thought, just someone getting home. But why not park in their driveway?

A door slammed, and he flinched, started to jog. The playground was closer now, half a ball field away. A curly haired figure sat on one of the swings, their back to him. Ellie.

Footsteps sounded behind him. Following him. His pulse spiked, and he tensed to run, to beat his best time on the hundred-yard dash, the three hundred. Hell, he could run a full mile without breaking a sweat.

Movement caught his eye. That swing, moving under the lights surrounding the playground, Ellie trailing her feet in the dirt.

He stopped. What if the weirdo behind him went after her, attacked her instead?

Paul whipped around, flexing his fists, already feeling the sweet sting of pain across his knuckles. "What's up, dude? You following me?"

The figure stopped and raised their arm.

A gun.

The thought barely registered before something hit Paul's chest. A sharp stab that turned the scream crawling up his throat into a hoarse gasp. He looked down, expected to see a hole gushing blood, but there was only a silver tufted cylinder. He swiped at the tube, unable to grasp it, fingers not working.

His head swam, and he went down hard, legs twisting awkwardly as he landed on the sidewalk. He wrenched his head to the side, staring into that dark and silent neighborhood, praying for a light to flip on. For someone to call out, to come help.

The person who'd shot him entered his vision, crouching beside him. They wore a mask covered in fur that featured a long, snarling snout and sharp teeth. A wolf.

"Why?" Paul asked, his tongue feeling swollen, covered in cotton. He managed to flail an arm, but his attacker swatted it away and leaned closer.

They held a long, shiny knife right up to his face, so it was all he could see.

"Don't make me use this, Paul," a deep voice said.

They know my name, he thought. His body was so heavy, and he wanted to sink into the ground, to let his eyes close, to go to sleep. All he wanted was his room, his bed.

"Mom," he managed, his voice cracking, before unconsciousness pulled him under.

TWO

AS THEY PULLED into the mall parking lot, Penny was struck by the eyesore that was the Eden Hills Fashion Mall. An homage to the 1980s and in-person shopping, the concrete, retro-futuristic shopping center boasted signs in pink and teal and featured towering glass and steel arches at each of the four entrances. To her artist's eye, the mall, her father's pride and joy, was ugly as hell.

Penny flipped down the passenger seat visor and leaned closer to the mirror to check her make up. Until recently, she'd embraced a natural look, showing off the freckles Becca said were her cutest feature. But B was in a new city with a new girlfriend and hadn't texted Penny back in weeks.

She had to admit, she liked the effect of her smoky eye makeup. It made her feel older, more sophisticated. Pulling out her strawberry lip gloss, she applied a thick layer, savoring the smell that triggered her craving for Jolly Ranchers. She pursed her lips and practiced her best flirtatious eyelash flutter.

"Who are you getting all made up for, Penelope?" Linda asked from the driver's seat of their new purple

Hummer. The color perfectly matched Linda's ridiculous double-breasted suit.

Penny angled a glare at her stepmother as she slid the wand back into her lip gloss and tucked it into the front pocket of her jeans. "I can't look nice for work?" she asked, her mind conjuring fantasies of being caught alone in the dark storeroom with her coworker, Dirk, the absolute cutest guy in school. If Becca could rebound, so could Penny.

Linda pulled into a space reserved for "Employee of the Month," though, as far as Penny could tell, her only job was to serve as brassy, blonde arm candy.

Penny hopped out, practically spraining her ankle disembarking from Linda's monstrosity of an automobile.

"Your father and I have plans after the ribbon cutting. Find a ride home, 'kay?"

"Whatever." Penny slammed the door and strode toward the east door, not waiting for Linda. Three years earlier, Penny's real mom died in a car accident, and her dad lost all interest in having a relationship with his daughter. All he cared about was the shopping center, his new trophy wife, and making money. Or at least she'd thought so until recently.

A cold wind whipped through the air, and gray clouds gathered on the horizon. Lightning flickered in the distance, and she pulled her cropped denim jacket closed as she surveyed the sky. She'd hated thunderstorms ever since she was a kid, when her dad would scare her with stories of Zeus, saying he sent lightning as a punishment for humans who went against his will.

A windowless, white cargo van with heavily tinted windows sat parked at the curb near the entrance, and Penny took a wide path around it, having seen enough serial killer documentaries to know one could never be too careful around vans.

Pushing her unruly, copper waves from her face, she entered the windowless mall and snaked her way through the throng of people. The inside resembled two oblong racetracks stacked on top of one another, highlighted by neon light trim in teal and pink. Massive white pillars ringed the lower-level track and supported the second story, and a pair of escalators connected the two floors at each end. One end of the loop featured a massive two-story food court, which her father owned, in addition to being one of the mall's main developers. It was his idea to celebrate the glory days of malls with the design.

Eighties pop music played on a constant loop from the speakers mounted to every pillar. "Fashion" by David Bowie played, barely audible above the din, and Penny walked in time to the beat.

An oval fountain stood in the center atrium on the first floor, surrounded by built-in stone benches where shoppers sat to take a rest or have a snack. The pedestal that rose from the shallow pool supported a bronze statue of the town's founders: three men in suits and bowler hats, one of whom was her great-great-grandfather. She watched as a little boy stood on the fountain's tiled, outer wall and tossed a coin high in the air.

People believed if you landed a coin in her great-great-grandfather's hat, which he held doffed in an apparent greeting, you'd be granted a wish. Penny remembered trying it herself, aiming for her ancestor's bowler and hoping with all her heart. But you couldn't wish the dead back to life.

Linda rushed past Penny, heels clacking on the tile floor as she raced toward Yarn Barn, the latest addition to the mall, located on the first floor past the fountain. A red ribbon tied in a bow spanned the store's entrance, and her father, clad in his typical bland-but well-tailored suit, held a pair of comically oversized scissors. He met Penny's eyes, and she raised her hand in a wave, which earned her a slight smile and a nod. Progress.

About the time everything blew up with B, she overheard him talking to Linda about how he wished Penny was more responsible, stronger. That pissed her off. But then he said he worried every day about her, that he was afraid he'd lose her like he lost her mom. So, Penny decided to try.

Linda sidled up between him and Mayor Aldrich, probably already planning to gush about how much she loved knitting, though the only things she ever crafted were cocktails. Mr. Lykoudis, Dirk's dad and owner of Lykoudis Construction, stood off to the side, arms crossed over his wide chest, a hard hat perched on his head. His company had built the mall and pretty much everything else in Eden Hills that was less than twenty years old.

A guy holding a camera topped with a bright light pointed it at the group, and a woman stepped forward with a microphone.

Penny's phone buzzed, and a selfie of her best friend Yelena lit up the screen, her charcoal-lined eyes wide in mock suffering. "Where r u? I'm so bored 😩," the message said. Penny smirked and replied, "OMW 😊" and shoved her phone in her back pocket.

Penny had originally planned to ask her dad to get her a job at the mall, but after overhearing his conversation with Linda, she decided it would look better if she took initiative and earned it herself. Luckily, Yelena put in a good word for her at Threadz, and Penny started work a month ago. Her dad had been impressed, seemed to be gradually lowering the wall he'd erected between them.

A woman darted in front of her, knocking her back and scuffing her new pink canvas sneakers. "Careful," she called, bending to pick up the piece of paper the woman had dropped—a yellow flyer featuring a picture of a smirking teenaged boy with messy hair and a simple wood cross on a chain around his neck. The headline read, "Have You Seen Me?"

She scanned for his name. Paul Shockley. Seventeen. Last seen almost a month ago. He was a year ahead of her, and she'd seen him around, though they'd never spoken.

Penny frowned, looked up to see the woman shove her way in front of the camera. Face etched with desperation, the woman grabbed the reporter's microphone and held up another of the flyers. Penny rounded the fountain, getting close enough to hear the woman's words.

"Someone must know something, must have seen something. He's a good boy. He wouldn't leave me," her voice cracked, and she started sobbing. "Please."

Penny's father stepped forward, his face creased with sympathy. He put his arm around her shoulder and turned her from the camera, steering her toward a young police officer who'd appeared out of nowhere, one Penny saw patrolling the mall to discourage the riffraff and nab the occasional shoplifter. Officer *Brady...Bradley...*something like that. He led the crying woman away.

"This is exactly why having places like Eden Hills Fashion Mall is so important," her father said to the camera. "We provide gainful employment to young people, help them become healthy, contributing members of society. We hope by providing a sense of community and purpose for our youth, we will discourage deviancy and do our much-needed part to help solve the runaway problem that has plagued our great town."

The reporter fired back. "But what do you say to those who don't believe all those kids ran away?"

Penny's dad blanched. "I'm not sure I understand."

"There have been more than two dozen disappearances over the last three years, all ruled to be runaways, but the parents of twenty-two of those children strongly believe that their kids did not run away, that foul play was involved. What do you have to say to them?"

Penny knew this was the question her dad feared most. After Agnes Gregory disappeared last winter, her father lost it at the vigil when someone called her a runaway. He was adamant that something bad had happened to his daughter, but no one seemed to agree at the time. Now, though, a lot of people were starting to wonder if the man had been onto something. Even Penny started to wonder. She and Agnes were in the same English Lit class, and Agnes had never struck Penny as bad kid, let alone a "deviant," and she certainly didn't strike her as someone who would just up and run away. Agnes was quiet and kind, and she seemed perfectly happy with her life.

Before Penny's dad could respond to the reporter, the mayor jumped in to take the microphone. "Now, we all know there's no evidence of that," he said, a placating smile on his face. "Eden Hills is a good community, and places like the mall provide a free, safe place for our kids to congregate. And if they, or their parents, should do a little shopping, spend a little money while they're here, all the better."

Her father smacked the mayor on the back, and they laughed.

Penny cringed, turning away to head toward the escalator. The civic leaders of this town may not take it seriously, but people at school whispered about some kind of killer, a monster snatching up kids. She crumpled up the flyer and went to throw it in the nearby trash can but stopped after catching sight of Paul's face peeking out from the crinkled folds. She sighed. *I hope they're right; I hope you really did just run away,* she thought, then stuffed the crumpled paper in her jacket pocket. It would be better for every kid in town if that was the truth.

THREADZ BOASTED CLOTHES in every shade of the pastel rainbow, showcased on faceless mannequins that dripped with complementary accessories of all sorts: purses, backpacks, jewelry, scarves, caps. Penny stopped to check her reflection in the glass of the store's window display. Her outfit was comprised almost entirely of clothes from the store, her old paint-covered overalls and peasant skirts, which she used to adore, now relegated to the back of her closet. It was time to embrace this new version of herself.

She looked at her phone and winced. Twenty-three minutes late. She hurried inside.

"Whoa," a voice said as strong hands grabbed her arms, halting her in place.

She looked up to find she'd barely avoided running smack into Dirk, whose face was now less than a foot from hers. Her earlier fantasy of getting trapped with him in the storeroom flashed through in her mind, and she worried that somehow, he could read her mind. "Uh, sorry," she said, sounding every bit as awkward as she felt.

He grinned, displaying the cutest dimples Penny had ever seen. Well, the second cutest. B had killer dimples. *Forget her,* Penny repeated to herself.

Dirk grabbed her hand, pulling her from the white-tiled center aisle that bisected the store and into the men's clothing racks. Heat flamed from the spot their skin touched, crept up her arm, up her neck. She'd always thought he was a bit of a jerk, but when she joined the Future Business Leaders of America, another bid to impress her father, he'd been the first to welcome her and offer his help.

"Look busy, bosses are here." He dropped her hand and grabbed a shirt from a circular rack, where it had been hung between pairs of Bermuda shorts.

She angled a look toward the back of the store, where Yelena's parents, Mr. and Mrs. Meyer, stood beside her at the island of registers in the middle of the store. They were dressed as if attending a formal event, Mr. Meyer in a blazer reminiscent of brushed silver, and Mrs. Meyer in a bold, red wrap dress. "Crap. I haven't even clocked in."

"They don't know that," Dirk said.

When the Meyers turned and headed toward the front, Penny grabbed a shirt from the rack closest to her and draped it over her arm. She pasted a smile on her face that she hoped would speak more of professionalism than panic and stepped into the aisle as they passed.

"Hi, Mrs. Meyer, Mr. Meyer." She hadn't seen them since they'd interviewed her for the position.

Mrs. Meyer's face crinkled into a genuine smile, and she pulled Penny into a mom-hug that loosened something in her chest. "How are you liking it here so far?"

"It's great. Thank you again for the opportunity." She almost blurted out that she'd been late but stopped herself.

"Of course, dear. Fay says you've been a model employee, not that we had any doubt." She looked at her husband, who nodded in agreement before glancing at his gold watch.

"We should go," he said. "Investors meeting with your father. We'll make sure to let him know how well you're doing."

"Thanks, I appreciate that." She gave a sheepish smile.

They left the store, and Dirk emerged from the racks. "Dude, *I've* never gotten a hug."

"Yelena and I have been friends forever, they're like a

second family to me." They'd gotten especially close when Yelena was in the hospital last year, but Penny didn't like to think about that.

He scoffed. "Why were you so worried about being late?"

Penny stepped back into the racks and rehung the shirt she'd grabbed, smoothing out the wrinkles. "I don't know, I mean, I want to do a good job, I guess."

"You need to chill out." Yelena walked up wearing one of the polo dresses they'd just gotten in, this one in lime-green, an outfit she wouldn't have been caught dead in a year ago. Back then, she'd despised all color. Her cropped black hair and heavily lined eyes were all that remained of her goth tendencies.

Penny rolled her eyes. "Spoken like someone who basically can't be fired."

"What can I say? It's good being the heir to a pastel fortune." She grinned. "I'm jonesing for a pretzel, come with me to Cousin Patty's."

The pretzel place was right next door, and Yelena ate there at least once per day. "I haven't even clocked in yet," Penny said.

"I did it for you after you texted. Now come on." She looped her arm through Penny's and tugged her toward the front entrance. "Tell Fay we'll be right back," she called back to Dirk.

"Only if you bring me a pretzel dog," he said.

"Yuck," Yelena said. "Doesn't he know those things are made of pig anuses?"

Penny giggled and leaned into her friend, happy to have Yelena back. She'd pulled away when she started working at the store, and Penny had been so wrapped up with B, she'd let it happen. But Yelena had still been the one Penny called when B broke up with her, the one who helped her make it through her first big heartbreak. Because best friends were forever.

THREE

"EDEN HILL'S FASHION Mall will close in five minutes," a voice announced over the loudspeaker, interrupting "Dead Man's Party" by Oingo Boingo. Penny grimaced as the lyrics told of a man dying from a lightning strike, all while the storm still raged outside, the crack and roll of thunder audible even through the dense layers of concrete surrounding her on all sides.

Threadz was almost empty, with the last remaining shopper checking out at the island of registers toward the back of the store. Fay finished the young woman's transaction with a cheerful, "Thanks for shopping at Threadz." After the customer left, Fay perched on a stool behind the counter and picked up her dog-eared copy of *Atlas Shrugged,* flipping the page.

Penny stood near the front display windows at a tiered table of men's polos, using a board to fold each one and stack them into piles according to size.

Yelena rolled by, using the fitting room's return rack as her own personal scooter.

"You're going to get in trouble," Penny said.

Yelena hopped down from the rack, tucking her cropped hair behind one ear. The silver charm bracelet on her wrist glittered under the lights, and Penny noticed a strange charm stamped with what looked like a capital P and an L combined into one. The symbol looked oddly familiar, but she couldn't place from where.

"Please. I'm fireproof, remember?" Yelena grabbed a mannequin with a teased-out brunette hairdo and pulled it from its stand. She held it close, clasping its hand and spinning in a circle.

Penny snorted a laugh. The change in her friend over the last year was amazing, and she had the mall to thank for it. Before opening Threadz, Yelena's family had been struggling to pay the bills and fighting nonstop. Now, they were all happier than ever.

As Yelena stuck her dance partner back on its stand, the brown wig slid from its head and dropped to the floor like roadkill.

Penny bent to grab the wig, and the balled-up flyer fell from her jacket pocket.

Yelena picked it up. "What's this?" She uncrumpled the paper, her brow furrowing.

"His mom was handing them out. She even interrupted my dad's ribbon cutting. Did you know him?"

Yelena was a year ahead of Penny, a senior like Dirk and Fay.

"Uh, not really. I mean, I had a couple classes with him." Yelena stared at the photo on the flyer for another second. She cleared her throat. "I…hope he's okay."

"It's weird, right? Another kid missing. What do you think is happening to them?"

"Closing time," Fay said as she walked past them down the center aisle, her perfect blonde ponytail bouncing with each step. She grabbed the hooked pole tucked in the front corner and used it to lower the metal gate that spanned the front entrance, then flipped the lock.

"What's happening to who?" Dirk asked, returning with an armful of clothes collected from the fitting rooms at the back of the store. He hung them on the rack Yelena had been riding.

"Paul Shockley," she said, handing him the flyer. "I guess he's missing."

"Yeah, missing." He snorted and balled up the paper, doing a lay-up to throw it in the trash can behind the checkout counter. "He just bailed like his deadbeat dad. Ellie's real messed up about it."

"Your sister?" Penny asked. Ellie was a junior, too, but she was a jock, like Dirk, so she and Penny didn't really run in the same circles. "They were dating?"

"Uh-huh. I say good riddance, though. She can do better than that loser."

Penny frowned. "But what if he didn't take off? I mean, what if something happened to him?"

"Happened to who?" Fay asked, returning from the front of the store.

"Paul Shockley," they all said in unison.

"Oh yeah, I heard about that. Another supposed run-away, right?" Fay crossed her arms. "I don't buy it."

"His mom doesn't either. She thinks something happened to him." Penny couldn't shake the image of that poor, pleading woman from her mind. "And what about the other kids? It seems like at least once a month someone goes missing. That's not normal."

"I'm sure the police are doing everything they can to find him though, right?" Yelena asked.

"Please. They're useless," Fay said. "Mayor Aldrich, too. I could do a better job than him." Everyone knew Fay had political aspirations, and Penny wouldn't be surprised if she ran for mayor after she graduated.

"Don't worry. If anyone comes at us, I'll protect you." Dirk draped a muscled arm over Fay's shoulder.

She rolled her eyes. "I can protect myself."

Penny frowned. Were Dirk and Fay dating?

"Enough chit-chat." She shrugged from beneath his arm and approached the registers. "Balance your drawer, then we'll start inventory. The Meyers want a shrinkage report tomorrow."

"You're not the boss of us, Fay," Yelena said.

Penny held back a smile. "Um, I think she is, like, literally the boss of us." Fay was an overachiever for sure—president of the student council and head cheerleader—but she was actually pretty cool to work with. She had taken extra time to show Penny how to make a schedule and submit payroll so she'd be qualified to be a lead herself, soon.

"Mellow out, babe." Dirk pulled a mini bottle of brown liquor from his pocket, cracked it open, and chugged. A sharp whiff of whiskey stung Penny's nose. "You guys ready for some fun?"

Yelena warned Penny that they usually turned inventory nights into an excuse to party, informed her that this would be her chance to prove that she could hang, even though she was a year younger. But if Mr. And Mrs. Meyer found out she was drinking at work, she'd be fired for sure, and all her efforts to show her dad she could be a responsible adult would be wasted.

"*Babe,* can we at least finish our work first?" Fay punched the buttons on the register, and her cash drawer popped out.

"I can't stay to hang out, sorry guys," Penny said.

Dirk's shoulders slumped. "That sucks, dude." He shook his head and followed Fay to the back office to lock up his drawer.

Yelena grabbed her arm once the others were out of earshot. *"He likes you, he likes you,"* she said in a sing-song voice. "He switched shifts to work tonight, you know. *After* he saw your name on the schedule.

"Yeah, right." Penny's face heated.

"I swear." Yelena made a little X over her heart with her finger. "Come on, you have to stay."

"My dad's just starting to thaw. I can't afford to mess that up."

"Please, you know he runs with Dirk and Fay's parents. He probably loves seeing you rubbing shoulders with them." Yelena grabbed Penny's hand. "And we have a solid nine months to make up for when I was hardly seeing you."

Penny's resolve crumbled. "Fine, I'll stay." Her dad couldn't be bothered to pick her up from work, anyway, so he would never know.

THE THREADZ STOREROOM was divided into two aisles by clothing-stacked metal shelves, and Penny, Yelena, Fay, and Dirk sat cross-legged in a circle in the center aisle with a cluster of mini bottles set between them. Dirk had flipped off all but one light, leaving most of the room blanketed in shadow. Penny's stomach gave a nervous flip when she took the whiskey Dirk offered her and their fingers touched.

"You couldn't have brought some schnapps or something?" Fay's mouth twisted as she eyed the little bottle in her hand.

Yelena cracked open her bottle. "Uh, no more schnapps. Remember what happened last time?"

Penny followed suit, opening her bottle as she watched her friend from the corner of her eye.

Fay sat up straighter. "That was *not* my fault. I thought the shelves were attached to the floor."

Yelena laughed, bumped Penny's shoulder. "You should have seen her. She tried to climb them, like all the way to the top."

"Only because *he* dared me." Fay mock-glared at Dirk.

"She almost got all the way up." He angled his head at the set behind him, closest to the wall. "That big gouge in the wall? That's where she hit."

"Good thing you're used to being the top of the pyramid." Yelena grinned at Fay. "You nailed that dismount. Besides, I kind of like whiskey. Burns good, you know?"

Penny laughed weakly, feeling like an intruder in this little clique. She and Yelena tried wine together once, sneaking it from her dad's massive stash, but that was the only time the two of them experimented with drinking. Apparently, Yelena had been having a great time with her new friends, experiencing all kinds of things without Penny.

The others held their bottles to the middle of the circle, eyeing Penny, who rushed to raise her own drink. "Cheers," they said, and drank their mini bottles in one slug.

Blowing out a breath, Penny followed suit, the fire of the whiskey blazing over her tongue and down her throat. She immediately started to cough, and they all laughed, Dirk reaching over to smack her back repeatedly.

"I'm fine," she managed, deciding that whiskey most definitely did not burn good.

"You're a lightweight," Dirk said, but with a good-natured smile. He wasn't wrong. Other than the one time she'd gotten tipsy with Yelena, she'd only ever had sips of wine or Champagne from her stepmom, who was constantly trying to share her drinks with Penny, to her dad's chagrin.

"Dirk's a pro," Yelena said.

"Like father like son, huh." Fay gave a nasty grin.

Dirk's expression darkened. "Screw you."

Penny had seen Mr. Lykoudis drunk once, when he and his wife attended a party at her house. He'd punched a bartender when they suggested he ease up.

"Not with how you're acting." Fay reached up to fiddle with the necklace that had been tucked into her collar, a silver chain and charm identical to the one on Yelena's bracelet.

"Hey, what is that thing?" Penny asked.

"What thing?" Fay said.

"That symbol you guys are wearing." Penny pointed to the necklace.

"Oh, um, it's a mall thing. Like, an anniversary gift once you've been here awhile." Yelena averted her eyes while shoving another mini bottle into Penny's hand.

She narrowed her eyes. Her best friend was lying.

Dirk winked and held up his hand to show a signet ring with the same symbol. "Don't worry, Red, you'll earn yours soon."

Her cheeks heated at the realization he'd given her a nickname.

"Come on. Drink." Yelena held out her whiskey.

Penny raised her bottle, then guzzled the liquor, the burn not quite as bad this time, her mind still locked on the strange symbol the others wore.

Her stomach gurgled and bile singed her throat. "Be right back." She got up and rushed toward the bathroom at the back of the storeroom, their laughter following her.

FOUR

WHISKEY DID NOT agree with Penny, but to her great relief, she made it to the bathroom before puking her guts out. Squinting against the too-bright fluorescent light that reflected off the white, tiled floor, she rinsed her mouth and patted the sheen of sweat from her skin before reapplying her strawberry lip gloss. She sincerely doubted there would be any kind of make-out session with Dirk, considering he seemed into Fay, but she still needed to find a mint.

Her gaze strayed to the quote painted on the bathroom wall, visible behind her in the mirror: ALL WEALTH IS THE PRODUCT OF LABOR —John Locke. Yelena's parents had stenciled the words there as motivation, but Penny questioned the choice every time she saw it. Hadn't they ever heard of TEAMWORK MAKES THE DREAM WORK? Or THERE IS NO I IN TEAM?

A muted scream interrupted her thoughts, and she shut off the water, straining to confirm what she'd heard. Another scream sounded, appearing to come from the other side of the wall by the toilet. Penny opened the bathroom door and peered out. Dirk, Fay, and Yelena sat at the end of the aisle where she'd left them.

The scream sounded again, louder this time, from the employee-only corridor that ran behind all the stores. Penny considered telling the others what she heard, but she'd already embarrassed herself by fleeing to the bathroom to hurl and decided to check it out herself first. It was probably just someone fooling around, anyway.

She crept toward the store's rear exit and pushed through into the door-lined corridor, a wide and high-ceilinged hallway used for deliveries. A guy in a yellow polo and visor that served as the uniform for the Cousin Patty's Pretzels next-door lay just a few feet away, curled into a ball on the concrete floor, with a pool of blood widening beneath him.

"Oh, God." She dropped to her knees beside him, tentatively touching his shoulder. "Are you okay?"

The guy rolled to his back, and she recognized him—Matt. He was on the football team with Dirk and had sold them their pretzels just hours earlier. A massive wound gushed blood from the center of his chest.

"S-stabbed. He stabbed—" Matt coughed, spraying her face in a mist of blood.

She pressed her trembling hands to his chest.

"Help!" she yelled, "Help us!" Someone needed to call an ambulance, but she knew she needed to keep pressure on the wound. It was bleeding through her fingers at a terrifying rate.

"Who did this to you?"

He grabbed her wrist and raised his head. "The…wolf."

"Wolf?" Her mind flashed to the images in her childhood copy of *Little Red Riding Hood.*

"Not done…said…he'll kill us all." His head fell back, and his arms went limp at his sides.

"Help!" she cried again. "Please, help us!" Couldn't anyone hear her screams?

With a hand pressed to Matt's heart, she tugged her cell phone from her back pocket and dialed 9-1-1 with one hand, smearing the screen with blood. The screen flashed, "CALL FAILED."

"Dammit." Her signal was never great in the mall, and the back corridors were the worst.

The rear door to the pretzel shop opened, and a guy rushed out, who she recognized from school but didn't know well—Jared. He wore the same yellow outfit and stared down at her with wide eyes. "Jesus. What happened?"

"Get some help."

"Jesus." Jared stood there, frozen.

Penny gritted her teeth. "Go into Threadz and tell them we need help. Now." She tugged her keys from her pocket and tossed them to Jared.

He nodded, fumbling before finally managing to unlock the door and wrench it open.

The seconds ticked by until the blood slowed to a trickle and Penny could no longer feel Matt's heart beating, or the rise and fall of his chest. Jared finally came back with Yelena, Dirk, and Fay, the group of them spilling out the door.

Dirk was laughing, probably assuming whatever he'd been told was a joke, but his good humor vanished at the sight of Penny. "Fay, call an ambulance."

"I tried, there's no signal," Penny said, her eyes fixed on Matt's face, which seemed too pale, too still. The pool of blood had widened to drench her knees and the toes of her shoes.

"It's okay, bro, hang on. You're going to be okay." Dirk knelt on Matt's other side, pressing his fingers to the boy's throat.

"I can't get a signal either," Fay said, holding her phone up as if that would help.

"I'll try the store phone." Yelena rushed back into Threadz.

"There's no pulse. He's dead." Dirk's voice was quiet.

"No." Fay shook her head. "Matt can't be *dead.*"

Penny pressed harder, willing his heart to resume beating. "Just call someone."

"I told you. It's not working." Fay gripped her phone tight.

Yelena came back out, panting as if she'd run. "The store phone is dead."

"What?" Penny's vision dimmed, a combination of panic and remnants of whiskey. "That's not possible."

"Let's get security. They'll know what to do." Dirk stood.

Yelena squeezed Penny's shoulder. "Come on. There's nothing more you can do for him."

She knew Yelena was right but hesitated, not wanting to leave poor Matt alone there, discarded in the industrial hallway like a piece of trash.

"We gotta go," Dirk said.

Her chin trembled, and she managed a nod, didn't trust herself to speak. Holding her dripping hands in front of her, she climbed to her feet, her sneakers slipping in the blood.

Jared steadied her by the elbow and handed her his apron. "Here. Use this."

Penny wiped her hands, staining the yellow red, and dropped it on the floor.

The stores were divided into sections, with a long hall running behind them, bookended by two short hallways that ran toward the interior of the mall in one direction and the freight elevator or loading bays in the other direction. The group followed Dirk to the fork that led to the interior of the mall, the only direct route to the corridor housing security.

Penny glanced back at her bloody footprints on the concrete, a fading trail of Matt's life.

Yelena came up beside her, hugging her close. "Hey, we're going to be okay."

"Not Matt," Penny said. Remnants of blood still streaked her fingers. She'd never had this much blood on her and wondered if it would stain her skin permanently.

"Do you know what happened?"

Unable to stand the sight of his blood any longer, she shoved her hands in her jacket pockets. "He said he was stabbed by the wolf, whatever that means. That the wolf wants to kill us all."

"The wolf?" Dirk asked, his voice sharp. "He said it was a wolf?"

"He was probably confused," Penny said. "I don't know."

"He's coming after us? Why?" Yelena asked.

"I bet this is what happened to all those missing kids," Jared said, pacing back and forth. "Some psycho has been killing them, but this time, we interrupted him before he could get rid of the body."

"Calm down," Dirk said, though his own breathing had sped up.

Penny laughed, the crazed sound bubbling from her throat. "There's someone running around killing people. What if he finds us? What if he gets us, too?"

"Freaking out won't accomplish anything. Get control of yourself." Fay pinned her with a hard stare, then looked at Dirk. "All of you."

Penny swallowed. She thought of her dad, of what he'd think if he saw her right now. He'd say she was too ruled by her emotions, too fragile.

Sucking in a deep breath, she said, "I'm okay."

"Come on, then," Dirk said. "And watch your back."

They exited into the mall's second story, careful to let the door shut quietly behind them. The normally lively space was dark, lit only by the lights that dotted the pillars along the metal balcony railing and the neon swooshes that adorned the balcony's perimeter. The sound system blasted "The Killing Moon" by Echo & the Bunnymen, the song filling the cavernous emptiness and making Penny want to smash the speakers to bits.

They crept past the dark and vacant stores, peering through the caged entrances of Barclay's Shoes, Books & Games Galore, Perfume Palladium, and The Candy Crossing. The shadows between island displays and racks of merchandise seemed to shift and sway, any of them potentially hiding the killer.

Penny knew she couldn't afford to fall behind, but she was paralyzed by fear. Her skin crawled under the invisible gaze of the man she was sure waited around the next corner. A rustling sound, barely audible beneath the music, pulled her attention behind her. A hunched figure rifled through a large duffel bag and placed something inside the manicured, potted bush at the base of a pillar fifty yards back. Focused on his task, whatever it was, he hadn't noticed them.

"Hurry up, or we're leaving you," Fay called.

"Shut up," Penny whispered, but it was too late.

The man stood. The light from the pillar acted as a spotlight, illuminating the matted fur and sharp fangs of the wolf mask that covered his face and glinted off the bloody butcher knife clutched in his hand.

FIVE

"RUN!" PENNY YELLED, plowing into the others and pushing them forward. Screams erupted as they caught sight of the killer. The others took off running down the second-floor walkway that stretched out ahead, but Dirk was frozen in place, staring at the Wolf.

"You…you're not… Who are you?" Dirk yelled.

Penny shoved him, propelling him after the others, and he finally moved. They were open targets for the killer, and she hoped all the wolf had was a knife. Behind them, he howled, and running footsteps sounded against tile.

With closed storefronts on one side and a railing that separated them from a thirty-foot drop on the other, they had nowhere to hide. They could keep running, but the walkway was one giant oval that circled the entire second floor, and the closest escalator was fifty yards away.

A kiosk of luxury hair products loomed ahead of them. Penny grabbed a bottle of coconut oil conditioner from the shelf without slowing and wrenched off the cap.

"I think your hair care can wait," Jared said.

Running backward, Penny squeezed out the contents of the bottle onto the floor, slopping a zigzagged line of the goop across the tile as the wolf man closed the gap between them.

She sprinted after her friends, risking a glance back over her shoulder. He hit the slippery patch and fell, but immediately got back up.

"What now?" Yelena asked between huffing breaths.

"Plan's the same. Make it to security." Dirk ran for the recessed door between two storefronts that would take them into the corridor that housed the second-floor security office.

A yellow "WET FLOOR" sign and a janitorial cart stocked with cleaning supplies blocked the entry, and Dirk shoved it aside to reveal the fallen body of a woman in a blue smock. One side of her head was bloody, as if she'd been hit or had fallen hard, and she stared up at them, her dead eyes wide and mouth gaping as if she might still scream. They all hesitated at the sight of the body, but Dirk recovered the quickest, hopping over her and pulling his keys from his pocket to unlock the door.

"Hurry," Fay cried, crowding Dirk.

He wrenched open the heavy-duty door and shoved Fay and Jared through, then grabbed Yelena's hand and yanked her toward him.

The wolf man plowed into Penny, and she went sprawling onto her stomach, her chin smacking the floor and sending pain radiating through her jaw. She flipped over to find the wolf standing over her, his knife raised. Pushing herself up into a sitting position and skittering backward until she bumped into the body of the dead woman, she watched him creep closer.

Dirk gave a cry and hurtled himself toward the wolf, attempting a flying tackle she'd seen him nail many times on the football field, but the killer picked up the wet-floor sign and whacked Dirk in the head, mid-air.

He crumbled to the ground, groaning.

Penny thought the wolf would stab Dirk, finish him off, but the guy seemed focused on her.

"I know you. Penelope. The daughter." He pointed his knife at her. "Another capitalism worshiping piggie."

Yelena cried out from the open door, reaching toward her friend, but Fay held her back. "You want to get killed, too, idiot?"

Penny reached out for the janitorial cart, grasping for anything that might serve as a weapon, as she kept her gaze locked on the killer. She snatched a spray bottle of cleaner and held it in front of her.

The man threw back his head and laughed, then bent down, weaving his knife back and forth. "You'll have to do better than that, little pig."

Dirk shook off the blow to his head and struggled to his feet as Penny pointed the bottle at the wolf and sprayed several times, aiming for the open eyeholes of the mask.

Howling, he stumbled backward, clutching at his face.

"You shouldn't get bleach in your eyes, asshole." She threw down the bottle and grabbed Dirk's outstretched hand. They barreled past Fay and into the corridor, the heavy metal door slamming and locking behind them.

Penny slumped against the wall, her chest heaving. Blood coated her mouth, and her jaw ached, but a quick probe with her tongue didn't find any broken teeth or other major damage.

Yelena hugged her tight. "I thought you were dead."

Penny patted her friend's back, swallowing down the blood tainting her mouth. "Saved by bleach."

The door shook in its frame as the killer yanked at the handle, then pounded on the metal surface. "I'll huff, and I'll puff…" he yelled, then broke into a maniacal laugh.

"COME ON." DIRK dashed down the short entry hallway, and they followed, veering left into the long corridor that served as the rear entry to the stores in this section of the mall. They slowed now that they were out of sight, and Penny eyed the doors, half expecting the wolf to barrel through one and ambush them. He didn't seem to have a key to the employee-only areas, but if he broke into one of the stores, he could come out the back way.

"That poor woman…" She pressed a hand to her stomach, knew she'd never forget the image of the woman's face, locked in a scream.

"Who was that?" Yelena asked. "Why was he wearing—"

"I don't know," Dirk snapped, and they lapsed into silence.

Halfway down the corridor, they reached the small, windowed security office.

Dirk pushed through the already open door and froze. After a moment, he stepped aside so they could all see inside. A desk with an empty World's Best Mom mug and a half-eaten sandwich sat below a bank of CCTV monitors that took up the entire side wall, the screens flipping between images from the hundreds of cameras placed throughout the mall. The wheeled desk chair had been tipped over, and lying on the floor was the gray-uniformed security guard, several bloody wounds marring her chest and arms.

"The wolf got her, too," Penny said, leaning against the doorway for support. If he'd gotten back here once, he could do it again. None of them were safe.

Dirk stepped over the guard, his white sneaker slipping in the blood and leaving a smear on the concrete floor. He picked up the phone on the desk and pressed it to his ear, then frowned and pressed the button several times. "It's dead."

"Kinda like us," Jared said, glassy eyed and only half-smiling. No one laughed.

"First the phone at Threadz, now this one. He cut the lines," Dirk said.

"Why? What does he want?" Fay asked.

"I think it's something to do with the mall," Penny said, and they all looked at her. "He knew my name, called me a capitalism worshiping piggie."

"Capitalism is the only moral system—" Fay started.

"Not now, Fay!" Yelena shouted.

"He's going to kill us!" Jared screamed. "Just like Matt, and the guard, and who knows how many others."

"No." Dirk smacked the desk with one hand. "We're going to find him and figure out who he is."

"Who cares?" Jared said.

"He's right, that doesn't matter." Fay gave Dirk a hard stare. "But we've got to stop him before he can hurt anyone else."

"What are you talking about?" Penny asked. "We need to get the hell out of here and call the police. Let them handle it. We should take the freight elevator down to the first floor and leave through the loading bays."

"What if there are others working late? They're sitting ducks waiting to be picked off," Yelena said.

"We can't stay here," Penny said. "And this place is huge. How would we even find him?"

"The cameras." Dirk faced the monitors, scanning the screens that flipped through deserted views of the food court, the east entry, the south escalator, and so on. "We find him, and we ambush him. There are five of us and only one of him."

"And we can keep trying to get the police, see if we can get a cell signal," Yelena said. "Or we can set off one of the store alarms. That'll get them to come."

"Good idea," Fay said. "We smash a few windows, and boom, alarm triggered."

"I don't know," Penny said.

"You don't want anyone else to get hurt, do you?" Yelena asked. "If we can help them, we should."

"We don't even know if anyone else is here," Penny said, but part of her wanted to find the guy and hurt him. Make him pay for killing Matt. Make him pay for forcing her to watch that poor kid die.

"We set off an alarm, then catch him ourselves," Dirk said.

"This is crazy," Penny said.

Fay put her hands on her hips. "Look, if you aren't up for this, you should go."

Penny winced, hearing her dad. He thought she was too soft, too much like her mom. If he were here, he'd be strong and decisive, find the killer and stop him.

"I'm good," she said. "I'm staying."

"I knew you had it in you." Fay gave an approving nod.

"There he is!" Jared cried, pushing past them and into the guard's office to point at the screen. The footage showed the guy, still wearing his wolf mask, striding past Candle Galleria on the first floor.

"What's he doing? I thought he was after us?" Penny asked.

"He probably moved on to someone else when he couldn't get in," Jared said.

"But he got in once and killed the guard." Penny watched him skulk across the TV screen, his duffel bag slung over one shoulder. "He was doing something out there in the hallway, taking stuff out of his pack."

"Maybe he wanted a snack," Jared said. "Killing's hard work."

"Whatever he's doing, it can't be good. We need to take him down." Dirk bent to unclip the guard's keys from her belt. "I have an idea where we can get some supplies."

SIX

THEY FOLLOWED THE corridor until they found the door labeled 'Kitchen and Bath Connection.' Dirk used the guard's keys and they all piled into the storeroom. A steady beeping sounded from the small, numbered panel on the wall. An alarm would activate unless they entered the disarm code.

"We tripped the motion sensor," Jared whispered, looking ready to bolt back out the door.

"We *want* the police to come, remember?" Penny surveyed the storeroom, which was much bigger than the one at Threadz. At least a dozen aisles of shelves filled the dim space and could have hidden a person from their view, but she reminded herself they'd been the ones to set off the alarm.

The group hurried down an aisle, past piles of dishes and rows of fancy olive oils, toward the door that led to the store's interior. Kitchen and Bath Connection was arranged into sections along each side wall, with freestanding displays dotting the middle of the central aisle that ran the length of the store. Lights in each of the four corners cast a minimal glow over them, barely enough to see.

Hooks at each section's partition held mesh shopping bags, and Fay grabbed one. "Come on. We need tape, rope, anything we can use to restrain this guy."

Yelena, Fay, and Jared walked off, intent on their assignments.

Penny's gaze strayed to the front gate. The mall concourse seemed quiet, no sign of movement between the store and the second-floor railing, but she knew the wolf could walk by and discover them at any moment.

"You need a weapon." Dirk grabbed Penny's hand and led her beyond the section of small appliances to the kitchen utensils. They walked past the boxes of dinner sets and glassware to the side wall and a mounted plexiglass case displaying a variety of chef's knives.

Dirk pulled a Leatherman from his pocket and busted the flimsy lock.

Penny chose a butcher knife from the display, testing the weight in her hand. Finding it too heavy, she opted for a large paring knife instead. An assortment of knife sheaths hung on hooks beside the display, and she grabbed one, ripping open the package and placing her new weapon inside the sheath.

Dirk watched her, his mouth tugging up at one corner.

"I mean, I don't want to stab myself if I have it in my pocket." She shrugged.

"Smart. You're pretty tough, too, huh?"

"Tough?" She scoffed. "I wish my dad could hear you say that. He thinks I'm a total wimp, that I just crumble under the slightest pressure." He never used those exact words, but he kept saying she should move on from her mom's death. And he'd been baffled by how upset she'd been after B dumped her.

Dirk looked at the ground. "Better than being a total screwup."

"Your dad said that?" When he didn't answer, she continued, "You're the one who's kept us all together tonight, who made a plan when we couldn't figure out what to do. He's an asshole."

Dirk gave a surprised laugh. "He can be, but, you know, he's my dad. Anyway, I'm glad you stayed."

"Thanks." She almost said she was glad, too, but she wasn't sure about that yet. "Sorry I lost my mind back there."

"First time you've seen someone die?"

"Yeah." She wanted to erase the image from her brain. "What about you? Have you ever seen…anything like that before?"

He looked away, not answering, and she wondered who he'd lost. "I think you were brave," he finally said.

"Not compared to you." She met his gaze. "I still can't believe it. How that guy could do something so…violent. All because he hates the mall, or something."

"This town would be nothing without the mall fueling our economy."

Penny huffed. "God, you sound like Fay."

He smiled, offering her a close up of those adorable dimples. "You disagree?"

"As my father says, the free-market economy is the engine of progress."

"Brains must run in the family." The smell of his pine-scented cologne tickled her nose as he leaned closer.

"Uh, yeah," she said, cringing. Real smart.

"We should hang out more, Red, get to know each other better."

She met his eyes, realizing how close they were standing, and that they were all alone. "Sure. I mean, yeah. We should." Warmth flooded her stomach.

Silence filled the air for a moment, then "True" by Spandau Ballet lifted from the speakers. She'd always thought the song was romantic, the kind of song you wanted to slow dance to.

Dirk reached out and tucked a rogue curl behind her ear. His touch sent a shiver over her skin, and he leaned closer, looking at her lips.

She raised a hand to her mouth, stopping him just a few inches away. "Um, I puked."

He blinked in confusion. "What?"

"Earlier. From the whiskey. I never got a mint." She backed away a few steps, her face flaming.

"Are you done over there? We've got to get going," Fay shouted from across the store.

Penny cringed, remembering how Dirk had acted with Fay earlier. "So, are you two a thing, or…?"

"Me and Fay?" he said. "Nah. I mean, we're not exclusive or anything."

"Does *she* think you're exclusive?" Penny arched an eyebrow.

"Definitely not."

"Uh-huh."

"Does that mean I get a rain check on that kiss?"

"Maybe. But if you tell anyone about the puke thing, I'll stab you." She held up the knife.

"Feisty, I like it," he said.

They started toward the others, but Penny stopped. "Wait, don't we need more weapons?"

"Get one for Jared. Everyone else should be covered."

"What do you mean?" she called after him, but he didn't answer.

Frowning, she grabbed another knife and sheath, then trailed him to where the rest of the group stood, near a display of holiday dishtowels in the rear of the store.

Yelena intercepted her. "What were you two doing over there, all huddled together?" she asked.

"Nothing. I swear."

"Ugh, your breath is rank." Yelena's nose wrinkled.

"I know," she said, somewhat glad for that fact. Had she really been about to kiss Dirk, who was only maybe single, with a psycho wolf on the loose and killing people?

"Okay, are we ready?" Dirk asked.

Jared opened the bag that was slung over his shoulder. "I've got twine and tape."

"Everyone have your weapons?"

Penny watched as, one by one, all the others except for Jared pulled out a dagger. Yelena bent down to pull one from her boot, Fay retrieved hers from her crossbody purse, and Dirk lifted his shirt to grab a blade from a sheath that was clipped to his jeans at the hip.

Setting down the knife she'd gotten for Jared, Penny grabbed Yelena's wrist and pulled the dagger closer. The blade was carved with several strange symbols that looked like runes, including that same P and L from the charms. "Don't tell me you all got daggers as a mall anniversary gift, too."

"Something like that," Dirk said with a smirk.

Jared frowned, more confused than even Penny, and extracted a Swiss Army Knife from his pocket. "This doesn't feel anywhere near as cool in comparison, but it does have a nail clipper."

Yelena caught Penny staring at her and said, "I'll explain, I promise. After we catch this guy."

"You better." Penny couldn't take her eyes off the ornately carved blade. What sort of twisted club had Yelena gotten herself involved with?

THEY RETURNED TO the security office, where the cameras showed the wolf man crouched at the bottom of a first-floor pillar, nearest the escalators at the north end of the mall.

"Let's get him. For Matt," Dirk said, and smacked Jared on the back.

Jared grimaced. "Alright. For Matt." He turned his yellow visor backward.

The best way to get the drop on the wolf was to approach from the opposite end of the mall, but they had to move fast. After sprinting to the south end of the second floor, they descended the immobile escalator as quickly as they could while staying silent.

The group of them snuck from one pillar to the next, using the tall, white structures and the potted bushes that accompanied them as cover. They crept past the fountain, the splashing water disguising the sound of their footsteps as they neared the wolf. Music spilled from the many speakers throughout the mall, providing a macabre soundtrack to their hunt for the killer. "Hungry Like the Wolf" by Duran Duran filled the air, and Penny hoped it wasn't an omen of things to come.

She'd been angry at the wolf man for killing those people, for making her watch Matt die, but the plan to apprehend him themselves seemed reckless now that they were so close. The others were way too calm, way too ready to take on a killer. Their composure, combined with the strange charms and daggers, suggested something sinister. But what?

The others closed in on the man, who was digging in the dirt of the one of the potted plants. Dirk took the lead, his dagger held ready at his side.

Penny rushed to the next pillar and took a deep breath, trying to slow her racing heart. She was tempted to run, to leave the others to their crazy plan. But what if Yelena got hurt? Or worse, killed? No way could Penny live with herself if that happened.

She would never forget almost losing Yelena last year after she'd taken some pills. It was Penny who'd found her and stayed by her side at the hospital; Penny who'd encouraged her to get treatment for her depression. When her parents bought the store and gave Yelena a job, she'd seemed happier than ever. Her family finally had financial stability again.

Penny leaned out to watch as Fay and Yelena ran side by side, their movements almost choreographed. Acid burned her stomach at the sight of them, so in sync. Yelena was *her* best friend, not Fay's. And best friends were supposed to tell each other everything. Once they got through this night—*if* they got through it—Penny was going to sit her friend down and make her spill her guts.

She peeked out again and saw she was three pillars away from the wolf man. Fay and Yelena were posted behind the next pillar, and Dirk and Jared were at the last one, their final hiding place before reaching the killer. Then, without warning, Jared stepped out and rushed at the man, giving a battle cry.

The wolf turned at the sound and raised his knife.

Seeing the weapon, Jared slowed and swerved so as to make a wide loop around the man and then accelerated surprisingly fast past the escalators and sprinted toward the darkened food court. Apparently, he'd decided that his attack plan wasn't such a good idea after all and chose to abort.

The wolf howled and loped after the teen.

Dirk shook his head in disbelief. Penny followed Fay and Yelena to where he stood, and he asked, "What the hell was that?"

"He's all-state track. No way that guy will catch him," Fay said.

"Do we go after them?" Yelena asked.

"No way." Penny put the sheathed knife in her pocket, done with this ridiculous plan that was sure to get them all killed. "We've got to get the police. Yelena, your car is here. Drive—"

"Wait," Yelena interrupted, tucking her dagger back in her boot. "The radio, we can use that."

Dirk slid his knife back beneath his shirt. "Right. Why the hell we didn't think of that before?"

"Guys, should we be talking about this, in, uh, mixed company." Fay shot a pointed look at Penny.

Penny threw up her hands. "Is this more of your super secret BS?"

"She's almost of age," Yelena said. "What difference is a few months?"

Dirk nodded. "I say yeah."

Fay huffed a sigh. "Fine. But if this blows up in our faces, I'm blaming you." She pointed her blade at Yelena, who just rolled her eyes and looped her arm through Penny's.

"You said you wanted to know our secrets. So, let's go." Yelena led her toward a recessed door between storefronts that led to one of the first-floor employee corridors.

SEVEN

FAY UNLOCKED THE door and held it open, gesturing for the others to enter before closing it behind them. The corridor had a similar setup to the one upstairs, with a short hallway that branched off to extend behind all the stores, except this hall continued past the freight elevator to a door that led outside to the loading bays and dumpsters.

"Where are we going?" Penny asked. When they turned where the corridor branched off, her better judgment urged her to run to the exit and then all the way to the police station.

"You'll see," Dirk said.

She glimpsed Yelena's bracelet again, glinting under the fluorescent lights. Penny gritted her teeth. She couldn't leave without knowing the truth about what Yelena had gotten herself involved with.

They reached a janitorial closet that sat on the opposite side of the corridor from the store access doors, and Dirk unlocked it. Shelves of cleaning supplies, several mops and buckets, a floor sink and other supplies filled the room, reminding Penny of the poor, dead cleaning woman.

Dirk stepped forward and opened a metal panel on the wall that looked like a fuse box. He removed his ring and pressed it, symbol first, into a small recessed circle at the bottom of the panel, below the two columns of switches.

Grinding gears sounded, filling the room, and Penny watched, open-mouthed, as the rear wall of the janitor's closet slid to the side to reveal an entryway and a large set of ornate, wooden, double doors at the end of a short hallway.

"What. The. Hell." Penny said. The charms and daggers were weird and a little scary, but the revelation of a secret passage spoke to this being much more than some weird club.

Dirk headed into the shadowy passage.

"I wanted to tell you *sooo* many times, but it's not allowed." Yelena grabbed her hand and dragged her into the darkness. "I mean, you would have found out soon enough. Technically the minimum age is seventeen, but you're super close, and of course you'd be initiated."

Penny struggled to comprehend what kind of high school club needed such a high-tech hidden room.

Dirk pushed open the wooden doors, which were carved with figures of ancient Romans in togas.

The doors opened to a large, well-lit, high-ceilinged room. At the center of the space, was a massive rectangular conference table inlaid with the same symbol from the charms, surrounded by tall-backed leather chairs. The two far-corners of the room had little seating areas with plush armchairs surrounding low tables. To her immediate right, another doorway opened to what looked like a commercial kitchen.

Fay pushed past to approach a small table against the wall that held a black box that looked like a scanner. She flipped a switch on the front and picked up the handheld microphone, pressing the side button with her thumb. "This is Fay Olson. I need to speak with Lieutenant Hewitt immediately. We have an emergency at the mall."

Tuning out Fay's voice, Penny circled the room, studying the photos that covered the walls, photos of people from Eden Hills: the founders, including her great-great-grandfather; the current and previous mayors; the developers of the mall, pictured at the ribbon cutting, including her dad, and Dirk and Fay's parents, who were the other investors; Yelena's parents in front of their store, smiling. A plaque read: THE FORTUNATE MUST NOT BE RESTRAINED IN THE EXERCISE OF TYRANNY OVER THE UNFORTUNATE. —BERTRAND RUSSELL.

Ruling over them all was a giant black-and-white painting of a Roman god with curly hair, a long beard, and flowing robes.

Penny began to tremble. "What is this?"

"It's the sanctuary, where we worship and atone," Yelena said, her voice almost cheerful.

Fay joined them. "The police are on their way."

"Thank God." Penny swallowed past the lump in her throat and eyed Yelena. "Worship what?"

"Plutus." She gazed up at the Roman god. "We are the Order of Plutus. And now, you finally will be too."

Penny stared at her friend, trying to comprehend the awe in her voice.

"You're freaking her out, Yelena." Fay led Penny the rest of the way around the room, as if giving a tour. "The founders of Eden Hills, our ancestors, knew they'd need an advantage to ensure their families were successful. And what defines success? Money, of course. So, they worshiped the most powerful god of them all, the god of wealth. Plutus."

Penny pressed a hand to her forehead, which had started pounding. "So, you worship money?"

Dirk flashed her a megawatt smile complete with dimples, but they didn't look so cute anymore. "What can I say? Greed is good."

"Have you been watching *Wall Street* again?" Fay asked. "He thinks he's Gordon Gekko or something."

Penny stared at the photo of her dad, realizing where she'd seen the symbol before. His ring. An heirloom he'd inherited from his father that was inlaid with black diamonds that distracted from the design: PL.

She started giggling and couldn't stop. So, they all worshiped money. Ridiculous, but people believed all kinds of weird stuff, and she already knew wealth was her dad's god. If they all wanted to chant over money and wave their daggers around like a bunch of weirdos, whatever.

"You okay?" Yelena asked, giving a nervous smile.

"Yeah. I just didn't know what to expect, I guess." Penny wiped her eyes. "I can't believe everyone who works in the mall is part of this."

"They aren't," Fay said. "Only a select few are chosen."

"Hopefully your dad isn't mad." Yelena cringed. "I'm sure he wanted to induct you himself."

"Me? Oh, uh, I'm sure it's fine." Penny furrowed her brow. She didn't say she had no interest in joining their weird order, because if it made her dad happy, she probably would, no matter how silly it all seemed. But she was a little hurt he'd felt like he had to keep all of it a secret from her, even if she wasn't technically old enough yet.

"You can't say a word to anyone outside the order," Fay said. "That includes Jared, when we find him. Got it?"

"Yeah, of course."

"Come on, the police are meeting us outside." Fay led the way from the room, Dirk pulling up the rear and closing all the doors behind them.

Relief slumped Penny's shoulders as they jogged away from the sanctuary and toward the exit door. Their nightmare was finally over.

EIGHT

PENNY STUMBLED THROUGH the door and into the loading bay, sucking in a deep breath of chilled, night air. Two cinder-block walls created an alcove that enclosed several dumpsters and cardboard collection bins, hiding the trash generated by the mall from the view of the customer. They only saw the neon and fountains and professionally pruned plants, never the detritus of consumerism. Penny almost started giggling again at the thought of asking Fay what Ayn Rand had to say about that.

The rain had stopped, but the sheen of it coated every surface and enhanced the rancid smell of rotten garbage wafting from the dumpsters. Her empty, whiskey tainted stomach turned as she rushed for the opening between the cinder-block walls.

The speakers mounted around the outside of the building ensured even those approaching the mall were inundated with the hits of the '80s, and "Don't Dream It's Over" by Crowded House lilted through the air. A siren sounded, the wail overtaking the swell of the music, and she watched a police car cut across the lot.

She jumped up and down, waving her hands. "Here! We're here!"

The black-and-white cruiser pulled to a stop just outside the loading bay, its headlights pointed at the exit door.

"We'll go talk to them." Fay gave Penny's arm a quick squeeze before leading Dirk over to the car, where an officer exited from each side. Penny knew their story sounded crazy, didn't want to be the one to explain what they'd seen tonight.

Yelena scuffed her feet on the wet asphalt. "Are you mad? That I didn't tell you about the order?"

"I don't know. Maybe," Penny said. "I mean, you're worshiping some Roman god now. And my father is too. It's…a lot."

"Greek. Plutus is—"

"Look, we can talk about it later." Penny looked down at her bloodstained clothes. "I just want to go home, take a shower, maybe try to sleep if I can." The images of Matt, the janitor, and the security guard looped through her mind, and she knew they'd invade her nightmares.

"It really has made my life and my parents' lives so much better. Your father helped us when we needed it. He's a great man."

"I'm glad, really." She watched the officers, who were huddled with Fay and Dirk, speaking in hushed voices. One of them, she recognized: Officer Bradley. He normally handled shoplifters and other troublemakers. Was he really qualified to catch a serial killer? "What are they waiting for? Jared could be hurt."

As if they'd heard her, the officers approached her and Yelena. Bradley gave a sympathetic smile. "Sounds like you've all had quite a night."

"Our friend is still in there." Penny gestured toward the door, wanted to tell them to hurry the hell up.

The other officer, who wore a patch on his chest that said Lieutenant Hewitt, said, "He'll be okay. We're going to make sure of it."

He had a kind face that was reminiscent of her grandfather, who'd died just last year. She wanted to believe him, but the wolf had killed at least three people tonight, and who knew how many before that.

"Get out of here. And make sure to call your parents if you haven't already." He looked at Officer Bradley and said, "Let's go."

She watched them go, taking in their immaculate uniforms and perfectly shined black oxford shoes that seemed like something her dad would wear. Eden Hills was a relatively small town, and they'd never had anything like this happen before.

"Be careful," she called, but they didn't answer, just drew their weapons and held them low as they advanced toward the entrance. Bradley unlocked it, and they both entered, letting the door close with a quiet click.

Dirk pulled a mini bottle from his pocket, cracked it open, and chugged it. He walked over to the dumpster and lifted the lid, tossing the empty bottle inside.

"What the hell are you doing?" Fay trailed after him. Penny and Yelena followed.

"Liquid courage." He blew out a breath and pulled out his phone.

Penny watched as he scrolled to the number for his dad but didn't dial. "Maybe you don't need to call him yet," she said, remembering Mr. Lykoudis punching that wall at her house. She wondered what he'd do if he thought Dirk hadn't handled things the way he should.

"It'll be worse if I wait," he said, staring at the screen.

Penny nodded and turned around to give him a little privacy.

"Want a ride?" Yelena asked.

"Yeah, probably." Penny pulled her phone from her pocket and stared at the screen. "I should call home first too."

"Let's not bring up the order," Fay said. "It would be best if your father doesn't find out we told you."

"I'm good with that." Penny was already nervous enough about explaining what happened, wondered whether her dad would approve of how she'd reacted. She'd tried to be strong, to do the right thing. Would he see that?

A quiet ring sounded behind her, and she looked over her shoulder, where Dirk stood with his phone pressed to his ear. But the sound wasn't coming from him. He frowned and lowered the phone slightly, then turned to follow the ringing, which appeared to be coming from behind the dumpster.

"Wait," she said, going after him.

On the other side of the dumpster, she found Dirk standing at the rear of a white cargo van that was parked in the shadows there, hidden from view. Dirk's hand hung at his side, still gripping his phone. The ringing was coming from inside the van.

Yelena and Fay joined them, huddling behind Dirk.

"What's going on?" Penny asked, her voice barely more than a whisper.

Dirk raised his phone and hit the "End Call" button. The ringing stopped. His phone slipped from his hand and hit the ground.

He reached for the rear doors, swinging them wide. The interior dome light flipped on, illuminating the back of the van.

THE BACK OF the van held no seats, just open space, and was filed with large paint buckets, scraps of wood, and several toolboxes. The scent of paint thinner stung Penny's nose, but there was another odor beneath it she'd already smelled too much of tonight. Metallic. Coppery. A little sweet.

A mound of something covered in a tarp took up a third of the space. Dirk grabbed the corner of the tarp.

"Wait." Fay reached out, as if to stop him, but it was too late.

He yanked the tarp free, and one of the toolboxes tumbled past the bumper to hit the asphalt with a crack that busted it open.

A moan escaped Penny's throat as her mind pieced together what she was seeing. Work boots. Jeans. A hand. Hair. And blood. Lots of blood.

"Dad!" Dirk half climbed inside the van and pulled the prone figure of his father into a sitting position, shaking him as if he might just be asleep.

Mr. Lykoudis's head flopped backward, revealing a deep slice across this throat that gaped open like a wide, toothless mouth, so deep it exposed a glint of white, bony spine.

Dirk pulled the body into a tight hug, uttering a muffled string of words Penny couldn't understand. She took a stumbling step backward and tripped over the toolbox, falling to the ground. Pain flared through her tailbone.

Yelena and Fay grabbed Dirk and pulled him away from his father, whose body slumped back onto the van's floor.

"Don't touch him," Fay said. "The police, they'll want to—"

"He did this." Dirk stood with his legs wide and his hands balled into fists.

Penny covered her mouth, held in the scream that wanted to escape. The wolf had gotten Dirk's father too.

"That mask. It wasn't just similar. It was my dad's. That bastard took it, and he…he…" Dirk's mouth moved, but he couldn't seem to say the last part out loud.

She frowned. The wolf mask had belonged to Mr. Lykoudis? The rain slicking the ground seeped through her pants, and she began to shiver.

"This can't be happening." Yelena crossed her arms over her stomach and swayed back and forth, back and forth.

Dirk stared into the back of the van, at his father's corpse. Tension vibrated through his body, every muscle tensed. His movements deliberate, methodical, he reached beneath his shirt and pulled out his knife, holding the blade up to glint in the moonlight.

"I'm going to kill him," he said, his voice flat, then spun on his heal and stomped toward the door they'd escaped through. Yelena and Fay chased after, yelling at him to stop.

Penny forced herself to rise to her knees, felt the dig of several sharp items that had spilled from the now open toolbox that carried the Lykoudis Construction logo. She reached down and picked up a wooden cross on a chain.

One she'd seen before. In Paul Shockley's photo.

She dropped the item as if it burned, and it landed among an assortment of other items. More jewelry, several phones, an inhaler. And a fountain pen with a name etched on the side. Agnes Gregory.

Penny scrambled to her feet, backing away.

A hand grabbed her arm, and she shrieked, but it was only Yelena.

"We couldn't stop him," she said, her expression pained.

Penny pointed at the items scattered on the ground. "This isn't right. Why did he have those?"

Fay strode up, tipped the toolbox upright, and began scooping the items back inside.

"Don't touch those—"

"We can't leave all this, the…the body, out in the open," she said, closing the box and tucking it back in the van beside the paint cans before slamming the doors closed.

Penny winced at the sound, which echoed through the quiet night. "Why did he have those?" she whispered. The evening's events scrolled through her brain. Matt, the cleaning woman, the security guard. None of it fit with the disappearances. And Mr. Lykoudis had a box full of random stuff. Of *trophies.*

The mall access door banged open, the metal smacking against the brick exterior, and Penny let out a startled scream.

"Dirk," Fay said, but it wasn't him.

Lieutenant Hewitt stumbled out, the bright fluorescents of the hallway framing him as he fell to his knees just past the door jamb, his body stopping the door from banging closed.

They rushed over to him, and Penny knelt at his side, her eyes locked on the red stain marring the side of his shirt, just above his waistband. "You're hurt."

He pressed his hand to the wound and groaned. "Bombs. He's planting bombs."

"We've got to get you some help." Yelena looked back at the police car.

"Already called in. On the way." He reached a weak hand up to the radio mic fastened to his shoulder.

"There's got to be first aid supplies in there—" Penny started.

"Listen to me," he barked, his voice commanding. "He's going to blow up the mall. Destroy it, destroy everything. You understand."

Fay stood. "We cannot let that happen."

"Where's Officer Bradley? And Jared?" Penny asked.

"Still in there," he said, wincing and falling back to sit against the door.

"Come on." Fay pulled the knife from her purse and stepped back into the hallway.

"We can't just leave him," Penny said, gesturing to the injured Hewitt.

Yelena tugged at her arm. "Help's on the way."

"Leave her, Yelena!" Fay shouted from inside. Footsteps sounded, running away.

"We can't let him destroy it. It's too important." Yelena's brow furrowed. "And the others could be hurt. We can't just leave them to die."

Penny stood, giving one last look at Hewitt, his face dotted with sweat. "We find them, and we get out. That's it."

Yelena didn't reply, just stepped back into the hallway.

NINE

YELENA AND PENNY entered the mall, both of them holding their knives out in front of them as they crept through the hall. Her hand trembled, the blade shaking.

"How do we even know where to go?" she whispered.

Yelena pointed to the drops of Hewitt's blood that led straight back into the heart of the mall. Fay was nowhere to be seen, but there were a few smeared tracks in the blood that could have been from her.

Penny sprinted up to where the hall split off, sucking in a deep breath before peeking around the corner. "Clear," she said.

Yelena rushed by, running with silent steps to the door that led from the employee-only area, and Penny followed. They reached the door, both of them panting. Yelena held up her fingers and did a silent count of three before pushing through the door and jumping out into the mall's first-floor concourse.

Penny piled out after her, leaving the bright fluorescents for the dim light of the sconces glowing on every white pillar, the neon accents, and the light that emanated from the fountain's floor, giving the water an eerie glow. A hand clamped over her mouth, and she gave a muffled scream as she was dragged backward. She sliced the back of her attacker's hand with her knife and twisted from their grip, turning to slash again with her blade.

Fay arched away, barely dodging the second attack. "Jesus, it's just me!" She licked the cut on her hand.

"Ew. Uh, I mean, sorry," Penny said.

"I'm fine." She lowered her hand, the cut still beading with blood. "Nice move."

"Why the did you grab me?" Penny asked, her heart pounding in her chest.

"Trying to keep you quiet," Fay whispered. "I heard something."

A howl sounded, and Penny spun in a circle, trying to place the location.

Yelena looked up at the underside of the second-floor walkway, which formed a roof over them. "He's above us."

"Hewitt mentioned bombs, could that be what he was putting in the planters?" Penny asked.

Fay pointed toward the escalators. "Come on then, we've got to stop him before he can destroy the temple."

"Temple?" Penny said, the disgust evident in her voice. "What about Jared and Officer Bradley? And Dirk?"

"This is more important than a few lives." Fay turned her glare on Penny. "If the temple is destroyed, there will be consequences."

"What, like Plutus will strike us down?" She couldn't help but be reminded of her father's stories of Zeus and his wrath of lightning.

"He could." Yelena averted her eyes. "And I don't know what the Archdeacon would do."

"Archdeacon? Who's that?" She remembered the photos from the sanctuary, figured it could be the mayor.

"Well, actually, it's your dad," Yelena said.

"My dad?" Penny gaped at her friend. "You're saying my dad is, like, the leader of your c—" She barely stopped herself from saying cult. "Club, religion, whatever you call it."

"This is your chance," Yelena said, stepping close, "to show him you're worthy."

"Worthy? Why would I—"

"I know you care about what he thinks, that you want him back, want things to be like they were before your mom…" Yelena swallowed heavily, didn't say the word *died* but Penny heard it anyway. "This is your chance."

She wanted to deny it, say she didn't give a crap what her dad thought. But she couldn't. As silly as the whole cult seemed, the thought of being excluded from it, of being written off by her dad once and for all, made her chest ache.

"There's Dirk," Fay whispered, pointing to the topside of the second-floor walkway visible across the mall's open center. He ran from one pillar to the next. "I'm going up to help him. You guys cover this floor."

She raced toward the escalator, her blonde ponytail a flashing beacon.

"You're not going to make me do this alone, are you?" Yelena asked.

"Fine. If we find him, we take him down." Penny only hoped they didn't get themselves stabbed in the process. "But if we find Jared first, or anyone else is hurt, we get them out of here."

"Fine."

They crept past the closed stores, peering inside each one to ensure they were undisturbed. Penny also kept watch on the wide-open space around the fountain. "Somebody's Watching Me" by Rockwell played, the lyrics narrating Penny's paranoia. The wolf could easily be hiding in the shadows in front of one of the stores, or inside one of them if he'd broken in.

Her own breath filled her ears as they moved along the loop of the first floor, her heart jumping every time they leapt past a blind corner or circled a kiosk that could hide the predator.

A rustle of fabric drew her attention to the mall's center, and she watched as a shadowy figure crept silently around the fountain. It was the silhouette of a man holding a gun. Officer Bradley. Yelena was several storefronts ahead of her, and Penny didn't want to risk calling out.

She raised her hands in the air, waiving them back and forth to catch Bradley's attention. He stopped when he saw the motion, then raced toward her. He pulled her into another one of the small alcoves that featured an employee-only door that led into the bowels of the mall.

"What are you doing here?" he asked.

"Hewitt said there were bombs, that we needed to help." She switched her blade to her other hand, wiping her sweaty palm on her jeans.

"You shouldn't be here."

"There's something else, something we found." She grabbed his sleeve, her words rushing out. "A van from Lykoudis construction. Mr. Lykoudis was inside. Dead. But there was other stuff, too, from those missing kids—I think. I don't know. Maybe Dirk's dad had something to do with the disappearances."

Bradley's shoulders slumped. "Damn it."

Footsteps slapped the tile above their heads. "Go. Get out of here. Now." He sprinted toward the closest set of escalators and crawled up the immobile steps, staying low to avoid being seen.

Yelena was a good forty feet ahead of Penny now and still hadn't realized Penny wasn't behind her. Penny watched as Yelena disappeared into a storefront that appeared to have been busted into, broken glass littering the tile floor.

"Hello?" A faint voice said. "Can anyone hear me?"

Jared. His calls seemed to be coming from the direction Yelena had gone, only much closer.

Penny took a step forward when a boom split the air and shook the floor, knocking her off her feet. A crack sounded above her, and she jumped back as a chunk of the ceiling smacked into the ground where she'd been standing. Several more cracks appeared above her head, spider-webbing the plaster, weakening it further.

"Oh, crap." She dropped her knife and raised her arms to shield her head.

SOMETHING KNOCKED PENNY off her feet, and she smacked her head on the floor. Her vision blurred for a moment, then cleared. A heavy weight sat on her lower legs. One of the pillars that had cracked in half had fallen onto her, but the plinthed end saved her calves from being crushed. Dust filled the air, blocking her view of anything more than a few feet in front of her.

She struggled and pulled but couldn't work herself free.

Another chunk fell from the ceiling, this one just a few feet ahead of her, but this time the debris was followed by a body. A quick flash of flailing arms and legs and a hollow "Oof" as they hit the ground.

She almost called out, thinking it could be Officer Bradley, then the figure sat up. The wolf, his furry mask covered in soot. Penny lay down, covering her mouth with her hands in an attempt to silence her panicked breaths.

The wolf coughed, and she lifted herself up just enough to see over the pillar that trapped her. He yanked the mask from his head and stood, slapping it against his leg to shake free the debris.

Penny gasped. She knew the man, had seen him at his daughter's vigil. Mr. Gregory. He looked different—his hair was longer, and his face covered in a scraggly beard—but it was definitely him.

He whipped his head in her direction, and she tugged harder at her legs, the ligaments in her ankles screaming. He stumbled through the debris, slipping but managing to stay upright, his mask still clutched in one fist at his side.

"You." He glared down at her.

"Don't hurt me," she said, her voice a whimper.

"Don't hurt you? Don't hurt *you?*" His mouth twisted in disgust. "My Aggie, my little girl, is dead."

"I'm so sorry." Hot tears streamed down her face. "Mr. Gregory, right? I knew your daughter. Not well, but I liked her. I had a class with her, English Literature."

He stilled, watching her, not moving.

She rushed on, "I remember she liked Thoreau. She wrote a story inspired by him. Something about birds, how they never sing in caves. She was really talented."

His eyes went glassy, and he cleared his throat. "You're her age. Too young."

"Yeah, yes, I'm only sixteen. Like her." Her lips began to tremble. She realized then why he would've killed Lykoudis, and she was glad he'd done it. Glad he'd stopped the man who was killing kids. "I'm so sorry."

He disappeared from view, and she held her breath, listening to his footsteps as he picked his way through the rubble, circling around to her.

A voice called out her name. Yelena. *Please, don't come back this way,* she thought. *Stay away.*

Mr. Gregory appeared near her head, a length of splintered rebar clutched in one hand.

"No, please." She pulled as hard as she could on her legs and managed to pull them a few inches farther, but when her ankle hit the unforgiving surface of the concrete pillar, all progress stopped.

Mr. Gregory knelt beside her, wedged the rebar beneath the pillar, then used all his strength to push down on the makeshift lever, his face reddening with exertion.

The weight of the concrete eased just a fraction, and she yanked her feet from beneath the pillar before he let it fall back into place. Penny rubbed her hands gingerly down her calves and winced at the tenderness there, at the faint hint of blood. No broken bones though.

"Damn cops messin' around," he muttered, throwing the rebar into the rubble. "Weren't supposed to go off yet."

Penny began to shake, aware of how close she'd come to having her legs crushed. She panted, the dust in the air seeming to choke her lungs.

"Whoa, now. It's alright, you're alright." Mr. Gregory crouched beside her, reaching out a hand but not touching her. "Deep breaths, now, deep breaths. In, one, two, three. Now out, one, two, three.

She forced herself to follow his count, again and again, until she finally felt normal again.

"I'm not going to thank you." She stood, wincing at the soreness in her legs but knowing it could be much worse. "After what you did to Matt, to that guard. Why? Why did you have to do that?"

He pulled his large hunting knife from a sheath at his hip, wiped the blade on his pants. "Wasn't personal. Got a mission, need to finish it."

"What mission?"

"Blow this place. Reduce it to rubble."

"Why, though? I don't understand."

His eyes filled with liquid, and a single tear rolled down the side of his face. "I hadn't been working in a while. Couldn't afford school clothes. Aggie just needed a few things, was growing out of her old ones. Wasn't her fault."

Penny struggled to follow his line of thought. "What? You mean she stole?"

"If I'd provided better for her, she never would've done that." He rubbed his chest with his palm. "Now she's gone."

She knew what he was feeling, that pain that seeped into your heart and never went away. "My mom died. It's been three years. And my dad, he's different now."

Mr. Gregory swallowed heavily but didn't say anything.

"I wonder sometimes, hope I'll see her again. You know, someday in heaven or whatever." She gave a half laugh, half sob. "God, that sounds so dumb, right?"

"No, not dumb." He cleared his throat. "Name's Howard. Never did care for mister."

"Howard." She swiped her forearm across her eyes, sniffed. "You really think Agnus—Aggie—would want you to do this?"

"Can't ask her, not yet. Maybe soon, maybe after." He pulled a little black box with a short antenna from a pocket in his cargo pants. There was some kind of cover over the top of a blinking light.

She'd seen enough movies to guess that it was a detonator, and took a step back, slipping on the rubble.

"I don't care about this place. But my friends… Enough people have died. Please, just let me get them out before—"

"Get outta here, girl," he said, sounding more tired than threatening. "Before my mercy runs out."

The dust was settling, their surroundings coming back into view, and she glimpsed her knife within the rubble.

He put the detonator back in his pocket and pulled the mask back over his head. The sight of that wolf face still scared her, but it also made her chest ache.

Yelena called out again, closer this time.

"Please, you don't have to do this," Penny said.

He pulled the hunting knife from the sheath strapped to his leg, holding out the blood-crusted blade. "If I don't, then it's all been for nothing."

A shadow appeared behind him, a flash of yellow in the darkness.

Jared leapt out, Swiss Army Knife clenched in one hand.

TEN

HOWARD TURNED TOWARD the sound, and Jared slammed into him in a flying tackle that would have made Dirk proud. "Leave her alone!" Jared screamed.

"No!" Penny lunged toward them, but they rolled, bashing into her injured legs. She cried out and lost her balance, landing on her butt. "Jared, stop!" she screamed, digging in the rubble and extracting her knife.

She crawled over the debris toward the two, wincing as the chunks of plaster and cement scraped her shins.

A yell sounded from above them, and Dirk dropped from the hole that had been blasted in the second-floor walkway. He grabbed Howard and pulled him off of Jared.

Howard took several wobbly steps backward in the debris, then regained his footing and lashed out not with his knife, but with his fist, nailing Dirk in the face.

Dirk cried out, and his nose sprayed blood.

Yelena emerged from the shadows at a sprint, and Mr. Gregory spun, swiping out with his knife and grazing her arm.

"Stay back!" Penny cried, climbing to her feet. Where the hell was Officer Bradley?

Dirk charged Howard, and they grappled, each gripping the other's knife-hand by the wrist. Penny edged closer, but hesitated, not wanting to hurt the grieving man who just wanted to avenge his daughter. Dirk slipped on a piece of drywall, and he went down hard on his back.

Howard stepped on Dirk's knife-hand, pinning it to the ground. Jared got up and ran at Howard, Swiss Army Knife held out in front of him, but Howard swatted it away, sending the knife to the ground. Penny rushed forward, and so did Yelena, but they weren't fast enough. Howard slashed out with his hunting knife, catching the expanse of Jared's throat. She reached the teen as he crumbled, caught him when he wilted to the ground, blood gushing from his neck.

Dropping her own weapon, she pressed her hands to his throat. She remembered the knife she'd gotten him, discarded on that stack of dishtowels when she'd seen Yelena's dagger. Why hadn't she remembered to give it to Jared? If he'd had a better weapon, he could've defended himself.

Yelena and Dirk got ahold of Howard's arms and pinned him to the ground. "Let go of me, you filthy little pigs," he said.

Legs appeared, dangling from the hole above them, and Fay dropped down beside the group. She helped hold the man's arms. "Get the rope." She pointed her chin toward the bag that had slipped from Jared's arm in the struggle.

Penny looked down to find Jared's lifeless eyes staring up at her. "No, no, no," she said, placing one hand on his cheek. He'd seemed sweet and funny and a little awkward. She wished she'd gotten to know him better.

Dirk let go of Howard's arms and stood but didn't make a move for the restraints. His eyes were wide, showing the whites, and his nostrils flared as he brandished his knife. Lunging so fast she hardly registered his movement, he stabbed Howard in the stomach, eliciting a muffled scream.

Penny's lips twisted in a sneer. *Good.*

Dirk knelt and pulled his knife free of the man's stomach to press the blade to his neck. In that moment, Penny wanted Howard to suffer, wanted Dirk to slice the dagger across the man's throat. His daughter dying didn't justify him slaughtering them all.

"Hey! You can't kill him," Fay said, her voice snapping his attention from Howard. "Dirk, you hear me?"

He froze, his whole body trembling, then finally pulled back. Turning away, he wiped the bloody blade on the tail of his polo, then stuck the blade back in its sheath.

The others tied up the wolf man while Penny carefully slid Jared's body from her lap. His ridiculous yellow visor sat cocked to the side in a way that seemed silly, would have made her laugh if blood weren't soaking his shirt and pooling on the floor. This was her fault. He'd died trying to protect her.

"Your dad begged and cried," Howard said, laughing in Dirk's face.

"You okay?" Yelena put a hand on Penny's shoulder.

"No." Penny stood, anger sizzling through her veins. "I don't know why you stopped. You should've just killed him," she said to Dirk.

"Don't be ridiculous." Fay huffed.

Penny grabbed her knife from beside Jared's body where she'd dropped it. "Jared was a good guy. He didn't deserve this."

"Calm down." Yelena approached Penny with her hands up to show her she meant no harm.

Penny's pulse throbbed in her ears. "You're not a hero, you know," she said to Harold. "You're a monster." She bent down and pressed the knife's point to the murderer's chest. One shove and she could skewer his heart. Penny yanked the mask from his head and dropped it to the floor, wanted to see his face.

"Guess we're all monsters." He gave a small, tired smile that seemed to accentuate his wrinkled, sunspot marred skin, the bags beneath his eyes..

Fay grabbed the roll of tape from the bag and tore off a piece, slapping it over his mouth. "Shut up."

"Try this instead," Dirk said to Penny. He kicked the man in the side, causing him to cry out from beneath the tape. "See? Fun."

Fay got in on the "fun" by delivering her own kick to the man's other side, right where he'd been stabbed. He gave another muffled cry, and she laughed.

Penny stumbled back a few steps, shaking. As angry as she was, she couldn't take pleasure in Howard's pain, didn't want to torture him. She turned away while Dirk and Fay continued their fun, the sound of their blows making her wince as if she were the one being kicked.

Her knees weakened, and she grabbed onto Yelena's arm to steady herself.

"I almost… I wanted to…" Penny shook her head, not wanting to say the words aloud, but unable to stop them echoing through her mind. *Kill him.*

Maybe Harold was right. They were all monsters. Even her.

Yelena gripped her elbow. "You okay?"

"Yeah." Blowing out a breath, Penny stood tall. There was a reason they'd come back inside the mall, and the sooner she could remind them, the sooner they could all get out.

She strode over to the next pillar and dug through the planter, peering through the fern's leaves at a chunk of what looked like gray putty connected to a small black box with several wires. "Hey, guys. Come here."

The others joined her, crowding around the planter.

"Should we try to disarm it or something?" Yelena asked.

"I think the cops were messing with them or something. That's what set the other one off," Penny said, not mentioning her heart-to-heart with Howard.

"Where the hell is Bradley?" Fay asked. "We need the bomb squad in here."

"Do we have a bomb squad?" Yelena asked. "And where are the rest of the cops? Hewitt said he called some in."

"We've got to get out of here," Penny said, her voice rising. "Whoever has a car, just go get it. We'll take him to the police ourselves."

"He stays here until those bombs are gone." Fay pointed at Howard, where he lay curled on the floor. "Insurance. He won't blow himself up."

"You sure about that?" Yelena asked.

"Then we take him to the Sanctuary." Dirk swiped the wolf mask from the floor, held it up to look at its face, then tucked it in the waistband of his pants, leaving the snout and ears to poke out from beneath his shirt.

Penny grimaced, knowing the mask had belonged to Dirk's father, wondering what he'd used it for.

DIRK GRABBED HOWARD'S bound arms and wrenched them over his head, tugging him along the floor. "Come on, grab his legs."

Howard pressed his lips together and his nostrils flared, as if he were holding back a scream.

Fay and Yelena ran down to the man's feet and grabbed his bound legs, following Dirk's path as he lugged Howard over the debris and toward the recessed door to the employee corridor.

Penny almost asked why they would want this bloodied killer tainting their sanctuary but decided she didn't care. If stashing him there meant getting out of the mall, that was fine with her. She cast one last look back at Jared's prone corpse before trailing after the others.

"Penny, grab an arm," Dirk said.

She caught up and gripped one of Howard's elbows so Dirk could move to the other side. Between the four of them, they lugged the guy through the recessed door and into the corridor. A low, wide dolly for hauling boxes sat next to the door for Craft Corner, and they put him on it. He groaned and pressed his hands to the spot where blood seeped through his shirt.

Dirk grabbed the handle of the dolly and led them down the corridor, turning at the fork and heading toward the janitorial closet. This time, Yelena opened the door by pressing the charm from her bracelet into the recessed circle, confidently, like she'd done it a million times.

A chill shook Penny, and she rubbed her hands over her bare arms.

The grinding gears sounded, and Howard wrenched his head to try and see the rear wall of the closet slide aside to reveal the carved, wooden doors.

Yelena proceeded into the short hallway and pushed open the doors to reveal the occult conference room beyond.

"I can hang back." Penny backed up, right into Fay.

"I don't think so." Fay pushed Penny, propelling her forward.

Dirk followed them, pulling the dolly inside and closing the doors behind them. Howard's eyes bulged as he took in his surroundings, and he tried to talk, but his words were unintelligible from behind the tape. Dirk, Yelena, and Fay stood silently, watching him.

"Okay. So, let's go." Penny gestured toward the door.

"Not yet." Dirk pulled out the mask and set it on a side table so it sat upright, staring out at the room with empty eyes. He drew his knife and pointed it at Howard. "You damaged our temple, killed Matt and Jared." His breath sped up, his nostrils flaring. "You killed my dad, you disgusting maggot—"

"Hold on—" Penny took a step toward him.

Yelena blocked Penny. "He's right. We have to appease Plutus, punish this vermin for what he's done."

She looked at Fay, the levelheaded one, the one who could talk the others down.

"We didn't stop him." She shrugged. "Sacrifice is the only way to atone, to make it right."

Dirk crouched, got right in Howard's face. "You're going to be the one to beg when I slice your skin from your body, cut your eyes from your head, amputate your tongue from your mouth. You'll wish you could scream."

"Take it down a notch." Fay nudged Dirk, and he scowled at her but stepped back. "We're not going to torture him. Much."

Yelena grabbed Penny's hands, locked them in a tight grip. "You understand, right? It's for the greater good, and he deserves it. He killed our friends. Tried to destroy everything everyone has worked so hard for here. Your dad. My parents. He wanted to blow up all our dreams, destroy everything."

Penny tugged her hands free, pressed her back to the door, the wood carvings digging into her shoulder blades.

"You're with us or against us." Fay took a slow step forward, reaching into her bag as she moved. A snake ready to strike.

"Time to choose, Red." Dirk met her gaze with flat, dead eyes.

A buzzing filled Penny's ears as the three of them surrounded her, closing in.

Howard looked between the others and Penny, then started to yell and bang his feet against the base of the dolly, drawing their attention.

That's when Penny yanked open the door, slipped through, and slammed it behind her. She knocked over the brooms and swept the supplies from a shelf to fall to the floor, hoping the muck would slow them down. The door to the corridor stood open, and she ran as fast she could down the hall and around the turn. She had to get to Lieutenant Hewitt, get help before they killed Howard. Before Yelena did something she couldn't come back from.

THE DOOR TO the loading bay was closed now, no longer propped open by Lieutenant Hewitt's body. She prayed he was still alive, waiting just beyond those doors, and that more cops had arrived.

She shoved through the door and stumbled into the night air, falling to her hands and knees on the asphalt. "Help, please!" she cried, raising her head to scan the loading bay.

A car sat parked several yards away, its headlights blinding her. She rose and stumbled toward the vehicle, blinking away the bright spots marring her vision. Two figures stood near the hood of the vehicle, a Hummer. Lieutenant Hewitt and her dad.

"Dad." She sobbed in relief and fell into him, her tears staining the fabric of his charcoal suit coat.

He hugged her tight, like he hadn't in a very long time, then pushed her away to arm's length. "Are you hurt?"

"No, I'm okay." She swallowed, trying to catch her breath. "You've got to stop them."

"The bomber?" Hewitt asked, wincing as he moved closer. His uniform shirt was unbuttoned, displaying the undershirt beneath, and the bandages covering his wound.

"We got him. But Dirk and Fay, they took him to the sanctuary. Said they're going to sacrifice him." She couldn't bring herself to include Yelena, knew her friend would never be doing any of this without their influence.

"Sanctuary." Her dad grabbed her arm and pulled her away from the Lieutenant, lowering his voice. "How do you know about that?"

"They told me, but that doesn't matter," she said, her voice rising. "We've got to get back there before they kill him. Please."

Hewitt strode up, re-buttoning his shirt. "Officer Bradley?"

"One of the bombs went off, I think maybe he was hit, but I don't know." She scanned the parking lot beyond, still saw only the one police car. "Didn't you call for backup or something? Where are they?"

"We can't wait," her dad said. "Let's go."

The passenger-side door of the car opened, and Linda stepped out, mouth gaping. "Penny?"

Her dad strode toward the door, Hewitt close behind. "Take her home," her dad said to Linda.

Penny's mouth went dry as she pictured them storming into the sanctuary, catching Yelena about to sacrifice Howard. Or worse, standing over his body. When Penny's mom died, Penny had pulled away from everything and everyone for months, drowning in grief. Her dad hardly mourned at all and lost himself in the mall development and finding a new wife. She never would have made it through that dark time without Yelena, who refused to abandon her. And after the breakup with B, she was there again, ready to pick Penny up.

She didn't care about Fay or Dirk, but she couldn't leave Yelena behind. Penny ran after the men. "I'm coming with you."

Lieutenant Hewitt held up a hand. "You've been through enough."

"Yelena's in there." She met her dad's gaze, not wavering or looking away. "Let me talk to her, see if we can avoid anyone getting hurt."

He narrowed his eyes, then gave a slow nod. "Okay."

"Where the hell are you going?" Linda called as Penny used her key to unlock the door.

"The sanctuary," her dad said. "Tell the others when they arrive."

Lieutenant Hewitt frowned, probably wondering what this sanctuary was, but didn't say anything. Penny felt a little bad for him and the other cops once they showed. Two serial killers, a bombing, and a secret hidden room was a lot for anyone to handle in one night.

ELEVEN

HEWITT LED THE way, inching along the blood-smeared corridor, his gun at the ready. Next came her dad, and then Penny. Music drifted down the corridor, quieter than it would be out in the mall concourse but still audible. The door at the far end of the short hall stood open, which allowed her to glimpse the bottom of the escalator and the corner of the fountain. As if the station had composed a soundtrack just for this night, "Livin' on a Prayer" by Bon Jovi filtered through the open door. She watched, waiting for someone to ambush them.

Mr. Lykoudis was dead, and Howard was out of commission, but she didn't trust Dirk or Fay.

They turned the corner at the junction that ran behind the stores and ran straight into Officer Bradley. He whipped around, gun raised. "Lieutenant." He lowered his weapon. "Sir, are you okay?"

Hewitt nodded. "You?"

Bradley was covered in dust and dirt from the explosion, had several cuts on his face, and his left arm hung at an odd angle. "I'll survive."

"Come on, then." Her dad passed the officers, leading the way to the sanctuary.

Penny's heart picked up pace the closer they got, her fear whispering for her to run away while she still could, to let Linda take her home, let her dad and the police handle this. But she resisted for Yelena.

They reached the janitorial closet with no problems. The supplies and brooms she'd knocked over were cleaned up and put back in their place as if nothing had happened. This time, her dad unlocked the panel with his signet ring, the one he'd inherited from his father that featured a PL, revealing the passageway and double doors.

Penny expected the officers to comment, but they said nothing, just entered the passage.

"Let me talk to them first. Okay?" She shoved by them.

"Keep them calm," Hewitt said. "Tell them you're coming in."

"Yelena, it's me," she called out, hoping her voice would carry through the thick doors. "Are you in there? Can you talk to me?"

The silence stretched until Penny almost couldn't stand it, but she forced herself to wait, her ears straining.

"I'm here," Yelena answered.

Penny's pulse spiked. "I'm coming in, okay? Just stay where you are."

Easing out a shaky breath, she let the officers pass her. They approached the doors, and Penny held her breath, dreading what they might find inside.

They swung the doors wide to display Howard stretched out spread-eagle on top of the conference room table. Two ropes bound him, each looped beneath the table to extend from wrist to wrist and ankle to ankle. He thrashed in place, tugging at the restraints and whipping his head back and forth.

She took several steps toward him, her eyes locked on the killer that was nearly a victim. Yelena hadn't done it. She hadn't crossed the line to become a murderer. Penny nearly sobbed in relief.

Yelena, Dirk, and Fay stood clustered together behind the table.

"I brought the police," Penny said. "They're taking him."

Voices sounded in the janitorial closet, and Linda pushed into the room, her eyes widening at the sight of the bleeding man strapped to the table. She was followed by Yelena's parents, who rushed over to her, Mrs. Meyer pulling her daughter close. Next came Fay's parents, who looked dressed for a formal event, he in a tux and she in a black floor-length sequined dress. Fay rounded the table to stand beside them on the side closest to the door, saying nothing.

Penny knew they were all members of the order, but who had called them? She glanced at her dad, but he just stood to the side, watching.

"My son, where is he?" Dirk's mom rushed into the room, her haggard face stained with mascara tracks. She ran to Dirk, who pulled her into a tight hug.

"Dad," he said, choking out the word.

"I know." She pulled back, placed her hand on his cheek.

"But I got him. I got him." He grinned, looking down at Howard.

"You're my good boy."

Penny cringed, tore her gaze away from the warped reunion.

Mayor Aldrich was the last to enter, clad in a bland brown suit. His eyes narrowed when he saw Penny.

The officers holstered their weapons but made no move to free Mr. Gregory.

"What're you doing?" She asked. "Take him, arrest him."

"I'm afraid not, Ms. Shultz." Mayor Aldrich stepped forward, his face set in a condescending smile. "I understand this man is a killer, and worse yet, he intended to attack the mall, to destroy our temple. The heart and soul of this town. We cannot let that stand."

"That's not how things work. That's not justice." She turned toward the officers again, then to her dad.

"Whose idea was it to induct my daughter into the order prior to the age of eligibility and without my consent?" Her dad looked to Dirk, then to Fay, who both averted their eyes.

"We had to tell her. We had no choice—" Yelena stopped talking when her father nudged her.

"What were we supposed to do? The police weren't showing up, and even when they did, they screwed it up and set off one of the bombs." Dirk fisted his hands at his sides. "We're the ones who actually caught this maggot."

"Mind your mouth, son." Lieutenant Hewitt didn't seem kind anymore, his smile having warped into something predatory. She used to see that with her grandfather, too, as if both men hid something sinister beneath the surface.

A shiver worked its way up Penny's spine as she realized not a single one of the adults was making a move to free the man bound to the table. None of them even seemed upset to see him there.

"Who is he?" Her dad angled his chin toward Howard.

"Howard Gregory," Mayor Aldrich said. "Was an enlisted man, artillery, but now he lives off the system like a leech."

A murmur of disgust traveled around the room.

"Dad?" she said, that single word a worthless plea against the truth she refused to accept.

"Give me a moment with my daughter." He steered her past the group and through the opening that led into the attached commercial kitchen, complete with walk-in coolers to the left, metal worktables bisecting the room, and the largest pizza oven she'd ever seen. Magnets affixed butcher knives and cleavers to the wall below a set of cupboards.

He opened the cupboard above the sink and took out a glass, filling it from the tap. "Drink this."

"No, I—"

"You'll feel better."

She grabbed the glass and threw it, smashing it on floor. The spilled water flowed across the tile to a drain. Among the bits of broken glass, she spotted what looked like a human tooth.

"You're a little old for temper tantrums." His mouth twisted in disgust.

She tore her eyes from the tooth, pushed thoughts of what they used this kitchen for from her mind. "That man. He's not the first, is he?"

"This may be hard for you to comprehend, but there are old ways, good ways, that are frowned on by so-called modern society. The paternal bloodline of our family has been ordained to keep those old ways alive." He touched the ring on his pinky. "While other religions keep their followers beneath their boots with demands of faith and offers of forgiveness and paradise, The Order of Plutus knows the truth. There is no afterlife, there is no paradise, except that which we create during our mortal lives."

"So instead of God, you worship money? That's not the 'old ways.' That's just capitalism." She'd gotten an A in economics, thank you very much.

Her dad gave a joyless chuckle. "And money is all that matters. Wealth makes the world go round, sweetie."

"You murder people," she whispered, forcing the words from her mouth.

"We give to Plutus so that he will bless us with prosperity."

"That's bullshit."

"Watch your language," Linda said, creeping into the room like some kind of lavender-clad cockroach.

"No way is some ancient god intervening to make you money." Penny sneered.

"Isn't he?" He cocked his head. "Malls are a thing of the past, the dinosaurs of modern America. All across the country they have withered and died, gone extinct. But because of Plutus, we have resurrected the dinosaur and made it stronger than ever. This place would be nothing without our sacrifices." His voice brimmed with pride, more pride than he'd ever shown any of her accomplishments.

"You can make money without hurting people, you know."

"Don't be naïve." Linda pulled a cigarette from her black Gucci handbag and lit it with a monogrammed silver lighter. "This is war. And in war, someone always gets hurt."

"Do you truly think that those who have nothing wouldn't kill to stand where we are, given the chance?" her dad asked, his tone too reasonable, his voice too calm.

"No. Killing is wrong, and there are plenty of people who would never kill anyone, no matter what. Not for all the money in the world."

"Would you? For all the money in the world."

"No!"

"So, you would rather let those you love suffer. And for what? Your morals? Your pride?"

"What? No. Of course not."

"Yelena, come in here," he called.

Yelena walked in, her shoulders slumped.

"Talk to her," he ordered, then stepped from the kitchen with Linda, waiting just outside the open doorway.

Penny could hardly look at the girl who was supposed to be her best friend, who she was supposed to know inside and out. The sleepovers, the late-night phone calls, the whispered secrets in the dark, it was all a lie. "How could you do this? Be a part this?"

"I had to."

"No." Penny's voice shook with anger, and she stepped closer to Yelena until they were only inches apart. "You had a choice. You *chose* this."

Yelena's brow furrowed. "You *have* no idea, do you? You've never struggled a day in your life."

"Don't change the subject. That has nothing to do with this."

"You're a spoiled brat." She jabbed her finger in Penny's face. "You've never worried about having enough food, about having a roof over your head, none of it. For some of us, having money is a matter of life and death."

"Oh, please. Stop being a drama queen."

"Remember last year? The hospital?"

Penny cringed at the memory. Yelena had collapsed, clutching an empty pill bottle, vomit dribbling from her mouth. "I thought you were going to die."

"My parents were fighting all the time. They wanted to get a divorce but couldn't afford it. They couldn't afford anything after my dad got hurt and the medical bills piled up. Our house was in foreclosure, did you know that? We were about to be homeless, on the streets with nothing."

Penny hadn't known it was that bad. "You didn't tell me."

"I was embarrassed. You have this perfect life." She sniffled. "The Order of Plutus saved us. Your dad saw what was happening and offered to help. My parents joined and opened the store."

"Help?" Penny scoffed. "He took advantage of them, manipulated them when they were desperate."

Yelena ignored her, continuing, "My parents were happy and fell in love again, and they loved me. We were a family, like before. When they told me about the order, and I saw all the good it had done, I knew I found a place where I belonged."

Penny remembered the change in her friend, and she had been so thankful for it. Seeing Yelena rise from that deep dark hole and start smiling again seemed like a miracle. But what she'd really seen was her friend being transformed into a brainwashed disciple. At least Penny realized the truth behind her friend's transformation before it was too late, before Yelena did something unspeakable.

"It's not too late. You haven't killed anyone yet," Penny said, lowering her voice. "You can still get out of this. I'll help you."

Yelena shook her head. "But I have killed. And I don't want out."

Penny backed away, bumping into the prep table. "You can't even kill a bug."

"I don't take pleasure in it." Yelena pressed her lips together in a grimace. "But I've done what was required in service to Plutus."

Penny's body went numb under the knowledge that her best friend, her sweet Yelena, was a cold-blooded killer. "Who? Who did you kill?"

Yelena swallowed heavily, opened her mouth, closed it. Finally, she said, "Addison Gregory."

"No, that was Mr. Lykoudis. I saw the van with his… his trophies…from the missing kids."

"He is—*was*—our hunter." Yelena focused on the floor, wouldn't meet Penny's gaze. "We must all make our offerings to Plutus."

TWELVE

THE TEARS PENNY had been holding back spilled down her cheeks. She wished more than ever that her mom was here. All Penny wanted to do was hug her right now and have her say everything would be all right.

"People die every day," her dad said, coming up behind her. "Murders, accidents, heart attacks, wars. Death is a natural part of life. Right and wrong are arbitrary constructs that change depending on what society thinks at the time. The only thing that matters, has always mattered, is power. And to have power, one must have wealth. It's always been that way, from the beginning of time."

She shook her head, knowing this wasn't her dad, not anymore. When she was little, long before her mom was gone, he'd been a good dad. She remembered them having backyard barbecues filled with laughter, him teaching her how to ride a bike and reading her bedtime stories of brave knights and beautiful princesses. But he hadn't been that person in a long time.

Pain spiked behind Penny's eyes, graying her vision. "I don't want to talk about this anymore. I want to go home." She wished she could forget this entire day.

"That's not possible. You must be inducted into the order. I'd hoped to wait until you were more mature, less… fragile." He frowned. "You've never been very stable. I suppose you take after your mother in that way."

"My mom was kind, generous, and loving." Penny's fists tightened and blood rushed in her ears.

He waved one hand. "You *will* be inducted."

"No." She exhaled slowly, tried to stop her heart from pounding.

"No one outside the order knows of our rituals, our beliefs. You will join."

"What if I refuse?"

Her dad's face tightened, and his Adam's apple bobbed.

Fay appeared, leaning against the door frame. "We'll kill you."

"Screw you, Fay." Penny gripped the metal prep counter, her knuckles whitening with the effort. "You'd never actually kill me," she said to her dad.

"I would hope you wouldn't put me in that position."

Yelena grabbed Penny's hand. "You're strong, so much stronger than I am. You can do this. I know it."

She extracted herself from Yelena's grasp. "What if you just let me go?" she asked. "I'll keep all this a secret. I won't tell anyone. I promise." Even as she said the words, she doubted them. A secret like that would be a cancer, eating away at her from the inside out.

Dirk stepped into the room, standing opposite Fay in the doorway, the feral smile of a jackal on his face. How could she ever have found him attractive? How could she ever have convinced herself Fay was a friend?

"That's not how it works. Once you know, you're either in or you're dead. Right, Mr. Shultz?"

Her dad sneered at Dirk, something unspoken passing between them.

Penny scanned the kitchen, looking for a way out, some escape. Past the cooler in the far corner of the room was a door, though she wasn't sure where it led. Maybe she could run. But then what? She'd have no family, no friends, no money. Nothing. Yelena was right. Penny was spoiled, had no idea what it took to survive without her dad's support.

"We'll just chase you." Dirk pulled out his dagger, pointing it toward the back door.

"And we will catch you," Fay said.

The two of them made the perfect, twisted couple. Yelena said she didn't take pleasure in killing, that she only did what was necessary, but Fay and Dirk seemed to enjoy it.

She looked to her dad. His face was completely expressionless.

Yelena grabbed a broom and swept up the broken glass while the rest of them stood in tense silence. Penny's dad stepped on the foot pedal of the garbage can against the wall, and Yelena dumped the glass and the stray tooth in the bin. When the lid closed with a metallic thunk, a memory surfaced in Penny's mind.

About a year after her mom had died, she'd talked her dad into getting a puppy, Wiggles. After the dog kept peeing in the house and chewing things up, he said he took the dog back to the shelter to be adopted by another family. But she'd seen what he'd done, though she'd told no one, not even Yelena, and time had managed to suppress the memory. Until now.

She was supposed to be asleep in bed but heard Wiggles yelp. She slid from bed and crept down the stairs, thinking he needed to be let out. Her dad stood in the middle of the kitchen, clutching the puppy's lifeless body in his hands. His face was calm, just like now, as he dumped the puppy in the trash, the lid closing with a metallic thunk. She ran back up the stairs and tried to convince herself he hadn't hurt little Wiggles. The dog had fallen, had some kind of accident. He was getting rid of the body so Penny wouldn't be upset.

Her blood cooled with the certainty that he would let Fay and Dirk kill her, or he would do it himself.

She was only sixteen, had her whole life ahead of her. Hell, she'd only had one serious girlfriend. She didn't want to end up like Jared, snuffed out before he'd even had a chance to grow up.

Penny didn't want to die.

Mayor Aldrich walked in the room, his face pinched with impatience. "Sir, we can't wait much longer. Lieutenant Hewitt needs time to devise an official explanation for all this before we call in the bomb squad."

Her dad shot him a look that made the other man back up a step, and Penny realized how much power her dad held.

He took her by the elbow, leading her back to the main room like the pawn he wanted her to be. "You're my daughter, and this is your birthright, your family's legacy. It's time for you to prove your strength."

Her dad never called her strong, and she cursed the pleasure that filled her at his approval. He was manipulating her, just like all the others.

But that didn't change the fact that she had a choice to make—between life and death.

He led her up to the table where Howard still lay, bound and struggling. "Will you join us?"

She only had one choice. Life. At least for now, at least for tonight, she had to cooperate. She wanted to live to see tomorrow.

"Yes," she said, bile stinging her throat.

YELENA STOOD BESIDE Penny, a smile splitting her face. At least someone was happy.

The others were quiet, regarding her with suspicion. She hated them all, but especially the parents. They'd brainwashed their children, turned them into murderers. Yelena, even Dirk and Fay, never had a chance.

"Penelope will be joining us, won't you?" her dad said.

"Yeah," she said, her voice hushed.

"Let's begin," he said, and everyone, even the police, took seats at the table, filling most of the chairs on either side.

Howard had stopped struggling, but the rise and fall of his chest showed his breathing had quickened. She wondered how much of their conversation he'd heard. Did he know Yelena killed his daughter?

Her dad gestured toward the seat at the head of the table, and she sat, perched on the edge of the chair as her dread turned copper in her mouth. Penny's mind whirled with images of sacrifices and rituals from movies. Howard would be killed, that much was clear, but she prayed she wouldn't be forced to help.

A sideboard with doors carved in those same Roman—no, *Greek*—figures sat against the wall, and her dad opened it to withdraw a small, rectangular, black wooden box that looked like a fancy jewelry case. He'd given her a set of pearls once in an identical box, but she knew this wouldn't be such a gift.

He set the box down and opened the lid to reveal a velvet lined interior holding an engraved silver dagger, like those the others had used in their hunt for Howard, except this one had a silver chain wrapped around the grip. He extracted the knife and set it on the table in front of her. The chain, he placed around her neck. She flinched as the cold charm settled on her bare skin.

She looked down at the emblem stamped into the surface of the metal.

"The overlaid P and L are the astrological symbol for Pluto. The Order of Plutus has used the sign to identify ourselves for generations. You'll wear it at all times."

The spot where the charm touched her skin itched, and she almost expected it to burn her flesh.

Her dad walked to the other end of the table and sat in the chair opposite her, at Howard's feet.

She watched as the others pulled something from the table's edge, gold coins that looked ancient, their surfaces carved with the head of a Greek god. Plutus, she guessed. They each kissed a coin, then touched it to their forehead and placed it on the table. The group turned to look at her, and she ran her hand along the edge of the table, finding a notch that held a coin. She pulled the coin free and kissed it, tasting acrid metal on her lips.

"Place your coin beneath the vermin's head."

Penny stood and placed the piece of gold beneath Howard's head, causing him to flinch. She couldn't help thinking about how scared he must be, tied to the table, helpless. Waiting to die.

"Venerable Plutus, revered by god and man, we submit to your rule," her dad said. "In your name, we amass wealth. By your will, we exercise power. Our dominion is in tribute."

"Hail Plutus," the group around the table responded. Yelena, Dirk, and Fay rose from their chairs and went into the kitchen.

Penny clasped her sweaty hands in her lap to stop them shaking.

A moment later, Dirk and Fay returned carrying silver trays holding flutes of what looked like champagne, and they set a glass in front of each person at the table, including Penny. Yelena followed with her own tray, placing a small white spoon piled with caviar next to each glass.

Penny thought drinking blood would be more appropriate than this. Champagne was for happy times, parties, celebrations. And the fact that they used that kitchen to store food, while also butchering people, curdled her stomach.

"We embrace that which you have given us, savoring the richest of delicacies as sacrament."

Each person picked up their spoon of caviar and ate it, many exchanging smiles of pleasure. Penny glanced at Yelena, who was licking her spoon as if it were the most delicious thing she'd ever eaten.

Her friend had probably never had caviar before joining the order. To Penny, it wasn't anything special, because she'd been afforded such delicacies her whole life. She picked up her spoon and gulped down the fishy roe, leaving a briny aftertaste in her mouth. She'd never understood the appeal of fish eggs. People only ate them because they were rare and expensive. A status symbol.

"Hail Plutus." Her dad raised his champagne glass.

She joined the others in raising her glass and taking a drink. Normally, she liked champagne, but not now. The bubbles stung her throat and settled in her stomach with the caviar, a sour reminder of the corruption she was now a part of.

"As we grow our wealth, so do we grow our numbers in worship of you." He reached into his jacket and extracted his own dagger, bigger than the others and more ornate, with a handle of ivory. He poked his middle finger with the knife's razor-sharp tip. Blood welled from the wound and dripped onto the table's surface, then disappeared.

A small lip around the perimeter of the table was pocked

with holes that lined up with each of the chairs, including the two empty ones. Her dad's blood had disappeared into a hole. But to where?

He cleared his throat, and she looked up to find him staring at her.

"Penelope Barbara Schultz, do you pledge fealty to The Order of Plutus?"

Internally, she pledged to only do what she must to get through this night with her life, but aloud she said, "Yes."

"Do you vow to honor the ways of the order and continue our traditions?"

Penny wanted to ask what those traditions were, make them explain what she was agreeing to, but it didn't matter. She'd agree to stay alive. "Yes."

"Take up your dagger."

She picked up the knife. The hilt was slippery, coated with her sweat.

"Venerable Plutus, our blood binds us to you in service." He gave a firm nod, eyeing the knife in her hand.

Trembling, she held up her blade. Yelena gave an encouraging nod and whispered, "You got this."

Penny stabbed her finger. Pain singed her nerves as the dagger split her skin, and she bit her lip. Her blood dripped onto the table and disappeared into a hole.

That was it. She was one of them now. Part of her expected a physical change to come over her, some sort of shift from normal girl to evil follower of Plutus, with pointed teeth and a voice that sounded of screams. But there was no transformation. She remained who she had been. A small relief.

Exhausted, she slumped in her chair, placing the knife back on the table.

Fay raised her eyebrows. "You're not done with that."

"He should be mine," Dirk grumbled.

"Quiet." Her dad stood and pointed with his dagger at the man tied to the table. "Venerable Plutus, Penelope offers this sacrifice to you in earnest, a demonstration of her loyalty, and in thanks for your continued blessings of wealth."

"What?" Penny's breathing picked up speed.

"An initiate must cement their binding with a sacrifice. Take up your dagger."

THIRTEEN

"MAKE YOUR SACRIFICE," her dad said, giving a deep sigh, as if he actually regretted making her do this. Penny wondered if he was thinking about his first sacrifice. Had he been scared too?

Howard tugged at his restraints.

Penny stared at her knife but didn't pick it up. She'd been so stupid to think she could get through this without hurting anyone. Yelena's comment about it being her turn pinged through her mind. "How many... times will I have to do this?"

"At initiation and periodically thereafter. With increased frequency comes increased wealth." He angled a look behind her, and she turned to see what she'd thought was a piece of art. A few dozen coins were affixed to the bare wall in a spiral shape.

She looked back at the coin that peeked from beneath the wolf man's head. Her vision swam, as if she might faint, and she fell back in the chair. So many lives taken, and for what? A fashion mall?

"If she chickens out, he's mine," Dirk said.

"And I get her," Fay replied.

Fay's mother gave a sharp, "Shhh."

"Penelope, Plutus requires sacrifice and does not wait for the faint of heart," her dad said.

She stared at Howard, at the grieving father who had gone mad trying to avenge his daughter. "Addison Gregory was his daughter."

No one looked surprised. They must have known.

"Why her? And Paul, and the rest of them?" She glanced at the wall, at all those coins, each one signifying a life taken.

"Thieves. All of them," the Lieutenant said. "They aim to take what doesn't belong to them, to steal from legitimate business owners that work hard and actually contribute to society."

"Shoplifters." Mayor Aldrich spat the word. "A scourge that have plagued malls for decades. But we won't stand for it in Eden Hills, won't allow it."

Howard shouted from behind his gag.

"Take the tape off his mouth." Penny said.

No one moved.

"I'm going to do this, but I want to hear what he has to say." And she wanted all of them to hear it, to have to listen to him. Especially Yelena. It was the least she could do for him now.

Her dad sighed, then gave a nod. Linda, who sat to Penny's right, reached out and tore the tape from the man's mouth.

"Children," Howard said, letting the word hang in the air. "Sometimes desperate, sometimes stupid, sometimes rash, but that's normal. They aren't less than anyone else, and they aren't a scourge. They're children! You've been sacrificing children!" he screamed.

Bile climbed up Penny's throat, burning her tongue.

"Many were, yes, but not all," her dad said. "We do not discriminate and get no pleasure from taking the young.

But those who would harm the mall must be punished. It is only fitting that they be offered to Plutus to ensure the mall thrives."

"Bullshit," Howard said. "You take those who won't be missed, those who can be explained away."

"You know quite a bit about the order, for vermin." Aldrich stood and pushed his own knife into Howard's leg, eliciting a scream.

Penny noticed her dad didn't admonish the mayor, was apparently fine with torture too.

"How did you come by all this information about the order?" her dad asked.

Howard said nothing as blood seeped from the wound on his thigh in a spreading stain.

"We clearly have a breach." Aldrich extracted his knife from the man's flesh and pointed at each person around the table, accusingly, the point of the blade dripping red. "And the only people who know of the mall's sacrifices are dead or in this room."

Each regarded the others with suspicion in their eyes as they tried to figure out which of them was a traitor.

Penny understood right away who it was, and so must the others. Officer Bradley wouldn't look at anyone, had focused his eyes on his lap.

The Lieutenant stood. "Bradley was responsible for collecting the names of the shoplifters. Compiling their home addresses after they'd been released from custody. Weren't you, son?"

"Yes, sir." Bradley got to his feet. Sweat beaded around his hairline, glistening under the lights.

"And I seem to remember this vermin coming into the station, making quite a fuss. Insisting his daughter wouldn't have run away. Who was it that talked with him?"

"That was me, sir, but I didn't say anything. I swear." He backed toward the door, one hand resting on his weapon. "I'd never do anything to harm the order."

The Lieutenant glanced at Penny's dad, who gave a nod.

Bradley's face blanched, and he bolted for the doors. He managed to grip the handle and pull one door open before a bullet hit him in the back.

Penny cried out and covered her mouth to hold in her scream, could only watch as Officer Bradley crumpled, rolling to his back and raising his arms as if to ward off the next attack. The Lieutenant calmly approached Bradley, raised his gun, and shot the young officer in the head. Blood spurted from the wound, expanding in a macabre halo.

"He was the only one of you worth a damn!" Howard yelled. "The only one who cared about my Aggie! The only one who cared about any of them!"

The Lieutenant holstered his gun and sat back down at the table, calm as if he were sitting down to dinner.

Mayor Aldrich shrugged. "I suppose that confirms it."

"It appears we owe you thanks, Mr. Gregory. You helped us root out a traitor in our midst," her dad said.

"Can we get on with this already?" Fay's mother said.

"Penelope," her dad said. "Take up your dagger."

Penny stood, bracing her arms on the table, afraid her legs might buckle as tremors wracked her body. Yelena seemed to be the only other person at all affected by Bradley's execution, her face pale and her breathing shallow.

Were they so used to witnessing death that they'd become immune to the horror? And would Penny become like them, too, someday?

Howard mumbled incoherently, half sobbing, the death of his accomplice draining his bravado.

"You've had your questions answered. I'll allow no further delays in the sacrifice," her dad said. "Pick. Up. Your. Dagger."

The caviar and champagne roiled in her stomach as she grabbed the knife, hating the feel of the hilt, the way it dug into her palm. She moaned and clutched her stomach with her free hand. Falling to her knees, she puked black fish eggs and sweet champagne all over the floor.

"Gross!" Fay cried, pushing away from the table.

The others reacted with equal disgust, except Yelena, who ran into the kitchen and came back with several towels. She crouched beside Penny, using a damp cloth to wipe her face. "The first one was the hardest for me, too. It gets easier, I promise."

Penny grabbed the towels from her friend, the words more disturbing than comforting. She didn't want it to get easier, didn't want to become numb to death.

"I'll buy you some time," Yelena whispered, then stood. "She'll be okay. Just give her a minute." She joined the others, who'd left their chairs and assembled at the opposite end of the room.

Penny crouched there, her dagger still clutched in one hand, and stared at the underside of the table. A network of clear tubes led from the holes in the surface to a large, gold bowl in the middle of the base. For collecting the sacrifice's blood. She didn't know what the blood was used for, but pictured those same champagne flutes filled with it, imagined the order members chugging down the viscous liquid and exchanging satisfied, red-lipped smiles.

She couldn't do this, even if refusing meant her own death.

Dabbing at her clammy skin, she noticed something else about the underside of the table. Right in front of her, at eye-level, the rope that bound Howard's wrists stretched taught.

Yelena talked loudly to the others, distracting them from Penny.

Not giving herself time to chicken out, she inched farther beneath the table until she was hidden from view and placed the towels over the vomit in the guise of cleaning up. Heart racing, she reached up with the knife and sawed at the rope. The sharpened blade took only three good swipes to sever the binding.

She got up and bent to whisper in Howard's ear. "Your hands are free. That's all I can do."

"Hey, what's she saying to him?" Dirk asked.

She knew that cutting Howard's hands wasn't enough. She had to do more if he was going to escape. "I told him I'm sorry about his daughter, but her death and his are for the greater good."

Yelena gave a relieved smile. "I told you she would be okay. She can do this."

"Sorry about that." Penny gestured toward the towels on the floor. "We were doing shots of whiskey earlier, and it didn't agree with me."

Her dad's brow furrowed, apparently able to disapprove of her drinking even during a sacrificial ceremony.

"I knew you were a lightweight," Fay said.

The others seemed to relax, and Penny joined them, standing with her back to the kitchen, drawing the focus to her and away from the table. "Dad, I know you've been patient with me, and I understand now. I want to join the order."

"Thank Plutus. I prayed you'd be stronger."

She frowned, wondering what he meant, then he hugged her. For a moment, he was the dad she remembered from childhood, not the monster he'd become. She returned his embrace, knowing it would be the last.

Over his shoulder, she watched Howard sit up and reach into the pocket of his cargo pants to withdraw a pocketknife and the detonator he'd showed her earlier. He sliced through the rope that bound his ankles and sat up.

"Hey, stop him!" Dirk yelled, alerting the rest of the group, who'd had their backs turned to the table.

Sitting on the edge of the table with ropes dangling from his wrists and ankles, Howard held up the little box. "Careful, piggies, unless you want to be blasted sky high. Can't spend all that blood money if you're in little bits."

The Lieutenant pulled his gun and pointed it at Howard but didn't fire. "Think he's telling the truth?"

Mayor Aldrich sighed. "Looks like a detonator."

"Kill him!" Dirk yelled.

"The temple must be protected," her dad said.

Penny knew they would shoot Howard in the back as soon as they had the chance, like Officer Bradley. Dagger still clutched in her hand, she pushed through the others.

"You'll get what you deserve, vermin," she said, putting herself between him and the group. "Go," she mouthed.

His eyes narrowed, and he snatched her wrist, pulling her back against him and circling her neck with his free arm. "You're coming with me."

PENNY GASPED AND dropped her dagger. She knew she wouldn't use it, couldn't use it, even if Howard did intend her harm. She wouldn't become a monster.

"Release her. Now," her dad said.

"I'll let the little piggie free once I'm clear of this place." He guided her backwards, stepping over the dead officer's body.

Penny took one last look at her dad and Yelena, tried to remember them as the best versions of themselves, before they'd been corrupted. She didn't trust that Howard would let her live, and part of her hoped he would be successful in his plan. So many kids had suffered at the hands of the order. Someone had to stop them.

"Close the doors," he rasped in her ear as they entered the passageway, loosening his grip enough for her to reach out and pull the door closed.

He released her and grabbed a broom from the janitorial closet. "Put this through."

She slid the wooden rod through the loops of the handles a moment before the doors rattled, yanked from the other side.

Limping, he stepped through the closet and peered into the hallway. "The coast is clear. Come on."

She followed, stepping into the empty hallway. "Let's Make Lots of Money" by Pet Shop Boys filtered through the corridor, and she huffed in disgust.

"Hey." Howard looked toward the fork in the corridor. "Go. Get out of here."

"Really? Are you serious?"

He flipped a switch on the detonator and slipped it back into his pocket. "You're not one of them." He pulled a small gun from that same pocket and checked the clip before popping it back into the weapon.

She knew he was a murderer, that he'd killed innocent people, but the order had forced his hand. He should pay for the lives he'd taken, but not as a sacrifice. "Come with me. We'll both go."

"Can't. Gotta be close enough to set off the charges." He gave a sad smile. "This was always meant to be a suicide mission."

"Do you have to do it? Kill them, I mean?" They'd done evil things, but she didn't want anyone else to die. "We could go to the police—"

"No one would believe us, and they won't stop. Next time, it'll be someone else's daughter." His mouth pulled down at the corners. "I'm sorry."

"Me too," she whispered, turning away. This was the chance she'd hoped for, to escape, and she had to go for it.

She'd taken only a single step when a door burst open about thirty yards away, blocking her path to the exit. The Lieutenant stepped into view, spotting them, and it was then that she realized where the door in the kitchen led.

Penny knew Howard had lost his leverage by putting away the detonator. "Grab on to me and run," she said, hoping the Lieutenant would be fooled, and she could buy Howard some time as his hostage.

He grabbed her wrist, tugging her along beside him.

They heard shouts behind them, and Howard fired twice at their pursuers. A girl cried out and Penny cringed, hoping it hadn't been Yelena.

They reached the fork in the corridor on the opposite end, and he pulled her right as shots sounded behind them. He stumbled and fell, crying out in pain. He'd been hit in the thigh, and the wound gushed blood, the widening stain enveloping the smaller blotches from the stab wounds.

"Get up." Penny yanked at his arm.

"Not happening. I'm bleeding bad." Gritting his teeth, he pulled out the detonator and pressed it into her hand. "Get to the center of the mall, close enough to activate the charges. Flip this switch to on, then press the trigger."

"What? No." She held the detonator with two fingers, afraid to even grip it. He'd taped a picture to the handle— Aggie's school picture.

He leaned away to fire into the hallway, earning another round of shouts, closer this time.

"I can't do this… It'll kill everyone. Me included," Penny said.

He deflated, slumping back against the wall. "You're right, you shouldn't die for this. Get yourself out. They'll know you helped me."

She stood, hesitating. "I'm sorry about Aggie."

"Me too. Now go." He winced and clutched his leg. "I'll buy you as much time as I can."

PENNY SPRINTED DOWN the hall, the detonator still gripped in her hand. Shots rang out and she pushed herself harder, faster. She made it to the door and burst through, exiting near the mall's center atrium.

She raced across the tile, eyeing the glass doors of the entryway past the fountain, just another fifty yards away. The expansive asphalt parking lots that stretched beyond the door taunted her, reminding her that there would be no place to hide once she was out, but she pushed the thought away.

The door slammed open behind her, and she dove behind the fountain, lying flat between the low stone wall of the pool and one of the built-in benches.

"Penelope!" her dad shouted.

"Come out, bitch. We know you were helping him," Dirk said.

"Shit," she whispered, letting her head fall back to bang on the tile.

"We're going to find you, kid," the Lieutenant called. "Might as well come out and make it easy on yourself."

Penny turned to look at the door to the mall, the same door she'd entered through just hours ago. The chance of making it out and across the lots before they shot her was slim. And even if she did make it, where would she go?

After being spoiled her entire life, taking everything she had for granted, it would be fitting to experience the other side of things. She wasn't sure she'd survive, but she refused to give up.

A figure darted from behind the escalators, forty feet away, on her side of the fountain. She was being surrounded, though no one had taken a shot at her yet. They hadn't seen her hiding between the bench and the pool, but they would soon.

Her chest ached with the certainty that she would never escape this mall.

The sound system went silent, then switched to the next song in an audio version of fireworks. "You Dropped A Bomb On Me" by The Gap Band played, raising a crazed giggle from her throat.

She eased up onto the ledge of the fountain, keeping her body pressed flat against the stone, then slid into the water, careful to keep the detonator above the surface. The pool was shallow, just a wishing fountain, allowing her to lie on her back without dunking her face. The sharp tang of chlorine stung her nose as she flipped the switch to activate the detonator.

"Please, Penny," Yelena called. "We can still figure this out."

Penny risked a peek over the top of the pool's edge and saw Yelena, side by side with her parents, all three of them carrying their daggers. Penny remembered so many wonderful nights with the Meyers, eating home-cooked meals or watching movies. They'd been there for her like no one else when her dad had pulled away. The order had turned them into strangers.

"Found her." Dirk jumped up on the wall of the fountain, now wearing the wolf mask. Ready to take his father's place.

"Wait!" she held up the detonator, the glowing lights a warning to her pursuers.

Her dad appeared at the end of the fountain to her right, Linda and the Lieutenant flanking him. He had shed his suit coat, exposing a wrinkled dress shirt stained with blood. His or someone else's, she wasn't sure. His carefully composed image was crumbling, revealing the rot beneath.

Penny stood, her soaked clothes sticking to her skin and shivers wracking her body. "Don't come any closer."

"You'd really do that? Blow us all up?" Yelena asked, edging up behind Penny's dad.

Fay scoffed, jumping up on the fountain's ledge, opposite Dirk. "No way. She's not a killer, remember?"

The Mayor and Fay's parents appeared at the opposite end of the fountain from her dad, their own knives brandished before them and feral grins on their faces that sat in stark opposition to their formal attire.

Penny pressed her back to the statue in the center of the fountain, letting the cold water drench her. The hand holding the detonator shook as she watched the order members creep closer. Her great-great-grandfather's statue looked down on her, and it crossed her mind to pick a coin from the pool and toss it at his hat to make a wish. But he'd never grant *her* wish—that The Order of Plutus had never been.

She whipped her head back and forth, watching the order close in from every direction. At the start of the night, they'd looked like the guests of some fancy dinner party. Now, their clothes were torn and stained, their hair was disheveled, and their masks of civility had fallen away to reveal the rabid monsters beneath. "Stop where you are! I'll do it!"

"I'd prayed you would be stronger than your mother. I take no pleasure in this, Penelope," her dad said, his voice breaking. "But I must do my duty to the order."

"Mom?" Her blood turned to ice in her veins.

"She was offered induction. She could have joined us, but she refused."

"It was a car accident. She was hit…" She struggled to breathe, pressed her free hand to her chest, certain her heart was tearing itself in half. "No. You wouldn't—"

"She chose to die," he said.

"You chose to kill her!" Even with all the evil she'd witnessed, she'd never imagined her dad could murder her mom.

Yelena and her parents had moved closer and stood right next to Penny's dad, but Yelena wasn't holding her dagger up anymore. It was dangling in her hand at her side.

"You knew? That he murdered my mom?" Penny screamed, brandishing the detonator, swinging it back and forth in front of her at arm's length.

"I didn't know. I swear." Yelena sobbed, her shoulders slumping. "I'm sorry. I'm so sorry."

"How could you do that? How could you kill her?" Penny's body shook, threatening to collapse. Her mom had stood up to him, stood up to the order, and she'd paid with her life.

"This is your last chance, Penelope. Hand over the detonator," her dad said, his voice emotionless once again, any regret over what he had done, what he was about to do, gone.

She realized he was the weak one, too weak to stand up for his own wife and daughter. Tears blurred her vision, and she blinked them away, let them drip from her face to mix with the water of the fountain.

Penny stared at the detonator, at Aggie's smiling face. She'd had her whole life ahead of her, but Penny's dad and his psychotic followers took that from her. From Aggie. From Penny's mom. From so, so many others.

She looked up to see her dad give a small nod to the Lieutenant, ordering the execution of his own daughter without a trace of regret. But before the Lieutenant could fire his gun, Yelena lunged with her dagger and stabbed him in the throat, causing him to fire wildly. A decorative silver orb hanging from the ceiling shattered, raining down shards of glass as the Lieutenant wilted to the ground, blood spurting from his neck.

"Do it, Penny, now!" Yelena yelled, then cried out, as if in pain.

"Get the gun!" her dad bellowed.

A dull ache radiated through Penny's chest, and she wished she could hug Yelena one last time. But the girl had fallen from sight, maybe dead, and Penny wouldn't be able to hold off the order members any longer.

"Screw your stupid mall, and screw Plutus!" she screamed, pressing the detonator's trigger.

A gunshot cracked and fiery pain slashed across her stomach a split second before the world exploded. Her legs went limp, and she fell into the water, rolling onto her back. A snatch of music swelled from the speakers, the last song they would ever play—"Cities in Dust" by Siouxsie and the Banshees.

Her mom's smiling face filled her mind, and Penny knew she was looking down on her, proud of who her daughter had become.

Above her, flames and smoke billowed through the air. Screams echoed through the cavernous space as a second round of explosions erupted, releasing shrapnel of metal and stone. Her vision blurred, and she winced at the pain in her side. She watched as the pillars that circled the mall's center cracked and tumbled down around them.

The second story seemed to disintegrate, the hand railing crumpling like paper. A rumbling crack sounded, as if the storm had returned with a roll of thunder, and huge chunks of concrete rained from the ceiling to expose the night sky, black as ink and shimmering with stars.

"We did it, Howard. We got 'em," she said as the pillar on the opposite side of the fountain crumbled. The stone monolith plowed into the bronze statue of the founders and sent them tumbling down on top of Penny.

EPILOGUE

"IT'S OKAY, HONEY. You're all right now," a deep voice said.

Penny moaned and cracked open her eyes, wincing at the pain that seemed to encase her entire body. She tried to speak, had to swallow several times before her voice would work. "Where…am I?"

"You're in the hospital."

She blinked repeatedly at the harsh fluorescent lights, took in the sterile white walls and scrub-clad nurse standing beside the bed to her left. Several machines sat behind him, one with a screen that blipped at each beat of her heart and another hooked to a plastic tube that snaked over the side of the bed and entered her arm. An antiseptic smell stung her nose, sharp but a little sweet.

Sunlight peeked through the drawn blinds on the windows that spanned the far side of the room, telling her it was daytime. But which day?

She tried to raise herself on her elbows but gasped and fell back at the burning pain in her side. The path of a bullet. With that, her memory came rushing back. "The mall," she said.

"You remember. That's a good sign."

"Did anyone else...make it?" Her breath quickened at the thought of her dad lying in a bed in the next room, waiting until he was strong enough to finish what he'd started, and she pressed her eyes closed.

"Rest now," the nurse said. "I'm going to tell the doctor you're awake. I'll turn on the television for you, but you just go on back to sleep if you need to. All right?" A soft click sounded, followed by muted voices.

Footsteps signaled the nurse leaving, and the door closed behind him.

Penny licked her lips, feeling the dry, cracked skin beneath her tongue. She raised her head, careful not to move too much. She was clad in a white hospital gown dotted with tiny blue flowers, and bruises in an array of yellow, blue, and black marred her arms. A cast encased her left leg, bulging beneath the soft white blankets that covered her.

The TV mounted in the room's corner was set to a news broadcast, and she squinted at the screen. The chyron at the bottom said, MADMAN BOMBS MALL, SEVERAL DEAD.

She reached for the remote on the small, rolling table beside the bed and turned up the volume. A reporter stood at the far edge of the Eden Hills Fashion Mall parking lot, several fire trucks and ambulances behind her. The mall had caved in on itself in multiple spots, the metal frames of the entry arches rising from the rubble like the legs of an insect.

"The town of Eden Hills is in shock today after forty-eighty-year-old Howard Gregory allegedly bombed the local mall. Police received calls late last night, stating a man killed several mall employees. After arriving on scene, the responding officers—plus several business owners and several mall employees—were caught in the explosion. A local teenager, whose name is being withheld at this time, appears to be the sole survivor of this horrific attack."

Penny clicked the mute button.

Turning on her side, she let the tears run down her face to soak the pillow. There, in a little glass dish on the table, sat her Order of Plutus necklace, blackened with ash. All that remained of her family's twisted life's work.

A soft rapping sounded on her hospital room door, and she sniffled, wiping off her face. "Come in," she said, her voice cracking.

"Hi, Penelope. I'm Dr. Patrick." A man walked in, clad in blue scrubs beneath a white lab coat. His graying hair was slightly askew, as if he'd given up on fighting several troublesome cowlicks.

She relaxed just a little in his presence. "I go by Penny."

"Okay. Penny, it is." He pulled up a rolling stool and perched near the bed, setting the chart in his hands aside and focusing his attention on her. "I bet you have some questions."

"I saw the news. They're saying I'm the only one left."

"They're still sorting through the wreckage, but that's what it looks like. I'm very sorry." The sympathy in his eyes weighed on her, something she didn't deserve, not after what she'd done.

"How did I...?" In those last few moments, watching the mall crash down around her, she'd been sure she was dead.

"My understanding is that they found you in the Founder's Fountain. The statue fell on top of you, protecting you from the blast and debris." He gave a small smile. "I guess your ancestors were watching over you from above, protecting you."

She wanted to laugh at the irony. If he'd had any power left, she was certain her great-great-grandfather would have killed her himself.

"Do you have any family I can call?"

"No." She swallowed heavily, missing her mom. "They're all gone."

"There are many kinds of family, you know. Those you are born into and those you choose." He glanced at her charm on the table, then tugged his own necklace from beneath the neck of his scrubs. A capital P overlaying an L.

She sucked in a breath and gripped the bedside railing. No, that couldn't be. She'd gotten them. Killed them all. She tried to speak but couldn't. Didn't know what to say.

"The Order is everywhere, all around the world." He smiled, patted her hand. "And you are part of our family. We're going to take care of you. Make sure you have everything you could ever want."

She fell back against the bed, her heart pounding hard enough to crack her ribs wide open. For nothing, it had all been for nothing.

"I know it's a lot to take in. Get some rest, and I'll be back later." Dr. Patrick stood and squeezed her shoulder. "Hail Plutus."

"Hail Plutus," she whispered.

Eden Hills Fashion Mall Playlist

1 Fashion
David Bowie

2 The Dead Man's Party
Oingo Boingo

3 The Killing Moon
Echo and the Bunnymen

4 True
Spandau Ballet

5 Hungy Like the Wolf
Duran Duran

6 Don't Dream It's Over
Crowded House

7 Somebody's Watching Me
Rockwell

8 Livin' on a Prayer
Bon Jovi

9 Let's Make Lots of Money
Pet Shop Boys

10 You Dropped a Bomb on Me
The Gap Band

11 Cities in Dust
Siouxsie and the Banshees

ACKNOWLEDGMENTS

I GREW UP in the '80s and '90s and was the quintessential latchkey kid, but the indoor kind. I wasn't into sports or riding my bike and didn't particularly want to be outside at all, so I spent many hours roaming the mall in my hometown (I can still hear the commercial jingle, "Meet me at Columbia Mall"). One of my first jobs was there, too, at the Spencer's Gifts. We mostly sold lava lamps, black lights, and Britney Spears posters.

It's interesting to me that malls have largely died, replaced by online commerce, but developers keep trying to raise them from the grave. Where I live now, our mall has been demolished and rebuilt a few times, the developers often incentivized by tax breaks and let off the hook via bankruptcy filings. Those developers seem to worship the almighty dollar above all else, kneeling at the alter of capitalism. *Chopping Spree* takes it a step farther, with *actual* human sacrifice needed to fuel the machine, but really, is the premise that far off from reality?

The original, shorter version of this novella was published by Unnerving Books as part of the *Rewind or Die* series. Looking back, that was a tipping point in my writing career. My first stand-alone book and the moment I started to believe I could really do this. I am so grateful to Eddie Generous and Unnerving for giving me that chance. When Rob, my editor at Dark Matter INK, suggested we expand *Chopping Spree* and re-release it, I jumped at the chance (and I'm forever grateful to Rob for his continued confidence and support). It allowed me to further explore a world and characters I really loved. Plus, I got to work with the incredibly talented Dan Fris on the new cover, which turned out absolutely gorgeous.

Thank you always to my partner, Zach. Remember our "fancy" dinners at the John Barleycorn? And grabbing Frosties at Wendy's, and playing air hockey at the arcade, and renting your tux for our wedding? Some of my best mall memories are with you.

Thank you to Meagan, Alexis, Saytchyn, and Tracy, who have critiqued versions of this story and helped it grow. And thank you to all my lovely friends and mentors in the writing community, as well as my friends and family back home. Your support keeps me going.

Lastly, thank you to my readers, those who read the original version and those who read this one. If you read both, I hope you found some new nuggets to enjoy. Some have asked if there will be a sequel to *Chopping Spree,* and while I don't have anything specific planned, I did leave the ending open to possibilities. To quote Romeo Void, "never say never."

—Angela Sylvaine

ABOUT THE AUTHOR

ANGELA SYLVAINE IS a self-proclaimed cheerful goth who writes horror fiction and poetry. Her debut novel, a '90s sci-fi horror comedy entitled *Frost Bite*, and debut short story collection, *The Dead Spot: Stories of Lost Girls* are out now from Dark Matter INK. Her short fiction and poetry have appeared in or on over fifty anthologies, magazines, and podcasts, including *Southwest Review, Apex,* and *The NoSleep Podcast.* She lives in the shadow of the Rocky Mountains with her sweetheart and three creepy cats. You can find her online angelasylvaine.com.

Also Available or Coming Soon from Dark Matter INK

Human Monsters: A Horror Anthology
Edited by Sadie Hartmann & Ashley Saywers
ISBN 978-1-958598-00-9

Zero Dark Thirty: The 30 Darkest Stories from Dark Matter Magazine, 2021–'22 Edited by Rob Carroll
ISBN 978-1-958598-16-0

Linghun by Ai Jiang
ISBN 978-1-958598-02-3

Monstrous Futures: A Sci-Fi Horror Anthology
Edited by Alex Woodroe
ISBN 978-1-958598-07-8

Our Love Will Devour Us by R. L. Meza
ISBN 978-1-958598-17-7

Haunted Reels: Stories from the Minds of Professional Filmmakers Curated by David Lawson
ISBN 978-1-958598-13-9

The Vein by Steph Nelson
ISBN 978-1-958598-15-3

Other Minds by Eliane Boey
ISBN 978-1-958598-19-1

Monster Lairs: A Dark Fantasy Horror Anthology
Edited by Anna Madden
ISBN 978-1-958598-08-5

Frost Bite by Angela Sylvaine
ISBN 978-1-958598-03-0

Free Burn by Drew Huff
ISBN 978-1-958598-26-9

The House at the End of Lacelean Street
by Catherine McCarthy
ISBN 978-1-958598-23-8

When the Gods Are Away by Robert E. Harpold
ISBN 978-1-958598-47-4

The Dead Spot: Stories of Lost Girls
by Angela Sylvaine
ISBN 978-1-958598-27-6

Voracious by Belicia Rhea
ISBN 978-1-958598-25-2

Grim Root by Bonnie Jo Stufflebeam
ISBN 978-1-958598-36-8

The Bleed by Stephen S. Schreffler
ISBN 978-1-958598-11-5

Saturday Fright at the Movies
by Amanda Cecelia Lang
ISBN 978-1-958598-75-7

The Off-Season: An Anthology of Coastal New Weird
Edited by Marissa van Uden
ISBN 978-1-958598-24-5

The Threshing Floor by Steph Nelson
ISBN 978-1-958598-49-8

Club Contango by Eliane Boey
ISBN 978-1-958598-57-3

The Divine Flesh by Drew Huff
ISBN 978-1-958598-59-7

Psychopomp by Maria Dong
ISBN 978-1-958598-52-8

Disgraced Return of the Kap's Needle by Renan Bernardo
ISBN 978-1-958598-74-0

Darkly Through the Glass Place by Kirk Bueckert
ISBN 978-1-958598-48-1

Soul Couriers by Caleb Stephens
ISBN 978-1-958598-76-4

Abducted by Patrick Barb
ISBN 978-1-958598-37-5

Little Red Flags: Stories of Cults, Cons, and Control
Edited by Noelle W. Ihli & Steph Nelson
ISBN 978-1-958598-54-2

Frost Bite 2 by Angela Sylvaine
ISBN 978-1-958598-55-9

Dark Matter Presents: Fear City
ISBN 978-1-958598-90-0

Part of the Dark Hart Collection

Rootwork by Tracy Cross
ISBN 978-1-958598-01-6

Mosaic by Catherine McCarthy
ISBN 978-1-958598-06-1

Apparitions by Adam Pottle
ISBN 978-1-958598-18-4

I Can See Your Lies by Izzy Lee
ISBN 978-1-958598-28-3

A Gathering of Weapons by Tracy Cross
ISBN 978-1-958598-38-2

Milton Keynes UK
Ingram Content Group UK Ltd.
UKHW041820210924
448622UK00004B/166